ENCYCLOPEDIA

ENCYCLOPEDIA

by Richard Horn

Tough Poets Press
Arlington, Massachusetts

Copyright © 1969 by Richard Horn.

All Rights Reserved.

No part of this book may be reproduced, for any reason, by any means, including any method of photographic reproduction, without the permission of the publisher.

Cover photo by H. Armstrong Roberts/ClassicStock/Getty Images

ISBN 979-8-218-12267-6

This edition published in 2023 with permission from the estate of Richard Horn by:

Tough Poets Press
Arlington, Massachusetts 02476
U.S.A.

www.toughpoets.com

In memoriam for Neal Cassady
(1926–1968)

Preface

In presenting this one-volume Encyclopedia, a concern for the modern reader has been the governing principle. Continuous change in the realm of knowledge is the unique heritage of contemporary civilization. An encyclopedist, in preparing a one-volume edition of general knowledge, should today have to take pains to discover recent developments in areas entirely unknown fifteen years ago, i.e., a new sun ship at Khufu, another comedy by Menander. This encyclopedia, however, is unique in two ways: It is not an encyclopedia or encyclopedic dictionary of general or specialized knowledge, but of particular knowledge, and it is not derived from any previous encyclopedia. Such a work is called on the Continent a hand encyclopedia. It should be noted here that although Europe figures in several important entries, the accent and style belong primarily to the New World.

We feel we have performed a service for the modern American reader by ordering the data of particular, daily life in a form already familiar in grasping the entire range of general knowledge (and most specialized fields), and thus affording the reader a new perspective from which, perhaps, he may better his understanding.

As we all have had occasion to consult an encyclopedia, no special comment is needed on the form of this volume. Certain specific usages, however, should be pointed out. Frequent abbreviations are used because of the repetition of many names and places, and to present the maximum information in the briefest space. In this book the cross-references are of the utmost importance. These cross-references are indicated by *ITALIC CAPITALS*. Furthermore, a person, place, or thing which has its own entry in this volume, when first mentioned in an entry other than its own, is in SMALL CAPITALS. The cross-references are not used recklessly; every possible effort has been made to guide the reader through *only* the relevant material, and to insure that the information under the other heading will be useful. As William Bridgwater once wrote, "It is easy to learn the method of following cross-references and gaining extra knowledge."

RICHARD HORN
Editor-in-Chief

Following is a list of names (words) and places abbreviated in this encyclopedia. Other words abbreviated in the text will be clear to the ordinary reader:

Comml. St. = Commercial Street
Hbkn. = Hoboken
mcg. = microgram
ms. = manuscript
N.Y.U. = New York University
Ptn. = Provincetown
Race Pnt. Bch. = Race Point Beach
Shankpntr. = Shankpainter
S.M.A. = San Miguel de Allende, Gt., Mexico
Wash. St. = Washington Street

A

ABORTION, self-induced by SADIE MASSEY (Aug. 3, 1966) in Ptn., Mass.; induced by an ampule (100 mg.) of ergotamine tartrate injected intramuscularly and pethadine, a synthetic morphine; Massey was assisted by TOM JONES, who believed himself responsible for the embryo. Massey said, "Up to two months this is the safest and easiest way. More girls should know about it."

AKTEDRON, given in answer to query by ALICE FAITH (Sept. 15, 1966) in Ptn., Mass., at the home of PETER PONZINI (See CONTROL YOUR DOWNS); Faith had asked: "What do they call Meth (methadrine) in Mexico?" (See SILVER EARRINGS.) The response came from an unidentified person. Faith inquired, "Do they have any rock music down there?"

ANDERSON, LANE (1931–), married, one child. State University College at Buffalo, 1300 Elmwood Ave., Buffalo, N.Y. 14222. 716-TT6-2320, ext. 685. Present home address: Box 4, Ridgeway, Ontario, Canada, 416-869-3238.

    B.A. Yale University, 1952, 80-page thesis, "Stephen Spender: A Study"; English Major, Philosophy Minor.

    M.A. New York University, 1958, 60-page thesis on John Millington Synge, "The Playboy of the Western World: A Misunderstood Classic."

    Ph.D. Expected New York University, 1966 or 1967. All

course work completed. 200 pages of dissertation completed: a critical analysis of Synge's *Works*, together with an examination of all relevant commentary and biography.

Fields of Major Concentration: Modern Irish Literature, Modern Poetry, the Romantics, Shakespeare, Non-Dramatic Elizabethan Poetry. Also have developed new method of teaching Freshman English: 16-page article on request.

1966–present: Assistant Professor, English Dept., State University College at Buffalo. Two World Literature Courses, Two Freshman English.

1962–1965: Instructor, Rutgers, The State University at Newark, Two World Literature Courses, Two Freshman English.

1959–1962: Graduate Assistant, New York University. Aided in new Freshman English Program with William Walker Gibson, continued Ph.D. studies under Profs. M.L. Rosenthal and David H. Greene.

1958–1959: Senior Street Gang Worker, New York City Youth Board. Working with juvenile delinquent gangs in East Harlem.

1957–1958: English Teacher, McBurney School, West Side Y.M.C.A., 15 West 63rd St., NYC. Five classes of English daily, taught swimming and diving classes, coached J.V. and Varsity Basketball.

1955–1957: Milford School, Milford, Conn. Six or seven classes English daily and Saturday, coached many sports, advised school paper and lit. mag., supervised dorms day and night.

Other relevant experience: Newspaper Reporter, 1965–66, Welland Evening Tribune, Welland, Ontario; 1947–52, The Daily Clarion. Radio Announcer, 1948–50, WSSV, Petersburg, Va., WMTR, Morristown, N.J.

Recommendations:

    Dr. Rogers Albritton, Head, Dept. of Philosophy, Harvard University, Cambridge, Mass., 617-868-7600.

    Dr. Benjamin Gronewald, or Dr. John Taylor, Dept. of English, State University College at Buffalo.

    Dr. David Sachs, Dept. of Philosophy, Cornell University, lthaca, N.Y., 607-AR3-4321.

    Dr. Jacob Lowe, Author and Educator, 50 West 69th St., N.Y.C., 212-MO2-6687.

Publication List (Poetry)

Arts and Sciences   Winter '63 (1)   "Bitter Little Metrics" (7)

Beloit Poetry Journal   Spring '59 (2)   "Getting Old," "Old Adolescent"

                                   Fall '62 (3)   "Irish Air," "At a Hoboken Ballfield, 5th and River Sts.," "In a Prep School"

Encounter (England)   Jan. '61 (1)   "A Dream of School"

                                   July '61 (1)   "A Fantasy"

Evergreen Review   Summer '60 (1)   "One Sentence"

Exodus   Summer '60 (1)   "Prayer" (from

Caligula, Canto XII)
(under pseud. Mike Shapiro, collab. w. G. Dennison, J. Raphael)

Inland	Winter '60 (1)	"Poem" (When I walk . . .)
Liberation	Dec. '59 (1)	"Lament" (I have married a transv . . .)
	Feb. '60 (1)	"Poem" (How happy those sons . . .)
	Mar. '60 (1)	"A List of Desires Frustrated"
	June '60 (1)	"American Boy"
	Nov. '60 (1)	"After a Visit to Children's Village, Dobb's Ferry"
	Jan. '61 (8)	"Little Prayer," "An Education," "Lower East Side," "Proctoring the Bio Exam," "Poem on 8th Avenue Between 42nd and 50th," "A Memory," "A Schoolmaster," "Poem (to P.G.)"
	Aug. '61 (1)	"Driving the Car with the Radio Loud"
	Sept. '61 (1)	"Description of a Photograph (in the *New York Daily News*, Nov. 3, 1960)"
	Jan. '62 (1)	"After Reading Paul Goodman's 'On Treason Against Natural Societies'"
	Sept. '62 (1)	"Seeing Things"
	Dec. '65 (1)	"A Reversal"
The Literary Review (8)	Spring '61 (1)	"Bitter Metrics"
	Summer '62 (1)	"John Hus"

MSS	Fall '51 (1)	"Katherine"

The Nassau Literary Magazine

	Summer '51 (2)	"A Drowning," "For N."
	Oct. '51 (3)	"The Mute Girl," "A Beddy-Bye in Gothic," "Distraction"
	Nov. '51 (3)	"Poem" (Nothing is amazing . . .), "Flight," "In Time of War"
	Jan. '52 (2)	"A Love Song," "Amaryllis"
	May '52 (1)	"Poem" (When I walk along . . .)
The Nation	Oct. 1, '60 (1)	"Lament for an Anger Unexpressed"
	Oct. 25, '60 (1)	"To a Used Auto Parts Dealer"
Outsider Shenandoah	Summer '62 (1)	"Lament"
	Winter '58 (2)	"An Envy," "An Old Tune"
	Spring '58 (1)	"Poems in Despair" (4)
	Spring '60 (3)	"In a Real Estate Office," "On a Poet Friend Who Recited Verses in a Police Station," "After Reading Kafka's A Dream"
The Spirit and The Sword	Dec. '65 (1)	"America, Spring 1965"

University of Kansas City Review

	Fall '55 (1)	"On a Young Diver"

ANDERSON, VALERIE (1943–)

Washington Square Journal
Dec. '60 (3) "Poem," "Description of a Photograph," "Aspect of the News"
Seeds of Liberation (Anthology: George Braziller, N.Y., Mar. 1965) (4) "Description of a Photograph," "An Education," "A List of Desires Frustrated," "Proctoring the Bio Exam"

ANDERSON, VALERIE (1943–), wife (and former student of) LANE ANDERSON; marriage in 1963 attended by their infant son, Lee; after death of parents in automobile accident in 1950, V. Anderson spent unhappy childhood in succession of Pennsylvania boarding schools; enrolled in undergraduate program at N.Y.U. (1959) where she remained for one semester; her household in Hbkn., N.J. was frequent gathering place for bohemian circle led by JACOB LOWE; love affair (1965) with TOM JONES, family friend and boarder, ended unhappily. (*See* THREE BOILED POTATOES.)

ANGRIE, EUGENE (1934–), Am. novelist and short-story writer; boyhood spent in Bklyn, N.Y., mother was a seamstress and took in laundry; left home at age 16 and traveled West and to Mexico (1952), supporting himself by such occupations as mechanic, photographer's model, dishwasher, etc. Began writing short stories in 1954 with encouragement from KARL SNIDE. Published first story in IMPARTIAL REVIEW in 1955. In 1958 his story "Pride" led to violent feud with BLACKY FALIS. In 1960 Angrie returned to live in NYC. His books include *Fat City Blues* (stories) and *Beefcake Boy* and *The Roller of Big Cigars* (novels). (*See* SNIDE, KARL.)

B

BASEBALL AND BULLFIGHTING, topic of conversation engaged in (July 9, 1966) between BLACKY FALIS and TOM JONES at the Old Colony Bar in Ptn., Mass.; after affirming a mutual enthusiasm for both activities, Falis told Jones he had almost remained in Mexico to write a novel about an American drifter from L.A. who becomes a matador. Falis expressed the opinion that a successful bullfight novel could be written in English providing the matador were an American. Otherwise, Falis assured Jones, the translation of every common object and occurrence into English from the original Spanish would be "too great a burden on belief." Falis continued, "I met this kid, Robert Ryan, who's trying to make it as a bullfighter down there. If he's given a chance to kill enough bulls he'll be alright. He has to fight deep prejudice and hostility, even to make it in the sticks. The remarkable thing is he's got to expunge from himself, with a cold scalpel, all the last endearing bits of his old, American ego and rebuild on just his guts and brains a whole new person to survive in a Spanish world, and in the arena." (Falis) Jones told Falis he had entertained fantasies about becoming a matador and playing major-league baseball. Jones held that each activity was an anachronism in its own culture, baseball for reasons of linear, sequential progression and bullfighting for the commercialism forced on it by the 20th century, which led through vulgarization to consummate decadence. Jones went on to develop the argument that the decline of baseball and "the corrida" (Jones) signified an end to the individualism and cult of personality which had lost its place in the American and Spanish cultures. Jones stressed certain physical parallels within both activities. He explained, "It's as if the man adjusts himself to the style of the moving object, in difficulty, grace, angle, position, etc. In baseball the first baseman will swoop down for a low, mean throw and stand normally upright for a straight peg at the shoulders. He's putting out more for the difficult, of course, but there's an aspect of each time harmoniously adapting to the style required by the moving object. The players assume an at-ease, hands-on-knees, posture before each play. It is the ability to adjust the style almost spontaneously to the random-changing pattern of the moving object that defines excellence. Now in bullfighting the moving object is the bull—*templar, rematar, lidiar,* are styles adapted to overpower the changing pattern of motion, i.e., to dominate the bull. The excellent matador literally adapts the natural style of the bull to his learned-artistic style. But at basis this must involve adapting to the style of bulls, since only for the bull is it natural. The adaptation or adjustment to the style of the moving object is common." (Jones) Falis remarked, "You rattled that off like a proof." Jones replied, "I know, that's the way it came out." Falis inquired of Jones whether he ever participated in these activities or only thought about them. Jones responded that he had played considerable baseball but had never caped a bull.

BEACON HOTEL, N.Y.C., on Broadway and 73rd St.; residence of SADIE MASSEY, who rented the penthouse; in Ptn., Mass. (Aug. 9, 1966), Massey and TOM JONES, who had shared residence with Massey in Beacon Hotel (*See BOX OF KLEENEX*), watched Chillerama, on Channel 7 (TV), Boston; mad doctor performed hideous brain operations in Beacon Hotel, finally destroying himself by detonating his penthouse laboratory. Jones and Massey agreed that they were well advised in leaving NYC for the summer: Jones added, "We really blew our minds in that hotel, Sadie."

BEADED NECKLACE (GLASS), made of antique beads dyed amber; belonging to SADIE MASSEY; when Massey took off the necklace (May 21, 1966) in TOM JONES's apt., she put it on his desk where Jones had left his poem STANZAS FOR THE SEDER. In the morning Massey discovered the poem and read it. Jones asked her whether she would like to have the original copy. Sadie Massey said she was unable to understand the meaning of the poem and suggested that Jones give it to a "more Jewish girl," (Massey) would be apt to enjoy it. Tom Jones said, "Ah, anti-Semitism rears its ugly head."

BEETHOVEN, portrait of, by J. Stieler, on wall of principal's office in Hbkn. High Sch., N.J.; HOBOKEN PARENTS FOR PEACE gathered there (May 9, 1965) under leadership of JACOB LOWE to protest air-raid drills of preceding day; parents with children in the school and other friends assembled in office to hear Lowe's address. Lowe spoke of urgent need to abolish drills on the ground that such exercises promoted a false understanding of the world predicament and that they instilled an imaginary security in the public mind. "We must help these children to become what they are, not foist our own meddlesome insecurities onto them." (Lowe) When he had finished speaking, the principal criticized Lowe for haranguing him, and said his views were "radical" and "baseless." He further added that, while some of the adults he recognized in his office had children in the school, others including Lowe did not. He questioned their right to petition in his office. While he was so arguing, JERRY DENFIELD, who was drunk, yelled, "I want to suck on the big cobalt beauty like a big tit." General pandemonium broke out in the office at this remark. When the principal attempted to forcibly eject Denfield, LANE ANDERSON, who was also drunk, pushed the man up against the wall with such force that the portrait of Beethoven was shaken to the floor. "You dirty Nazi crum, take that!" shouted Lane Anderson in the principal's face. Jacob Lowe, who had observed the proceedings with utter chagrin, deplored aloud to the ceiling, "A whole generation of the best." (*See DUNHILL PIPESTEM.*)

BIO-CYBERNETIC BRAIN PACK, referred to by SADIE MASSEY in conversation with BLACKY FALIS (Aug. 24, 1966), in Ptn., Mass., at the Falis home on Shankpntr. Rd.; Massey said that the Russians had been working on such a device to be operational by 1985. It would involve cybernetic programming and transmission of material to the storage areas of the brain. The "pack" would contain interchangeable cartridges, each containing the total comprehensible knowledge of a given area. Sadie Massey said, "You could free your brain to begin at the conceptual level. You wouldn't have to do all the busywork of finding out. Whatever you were interested in, you could find out about it in the brain pack, and it would be just like you always knew it. You could just expand and expand and expand." (Massey)

BISHOP'S COPE (a long cloak made of semicircular black satin, with embroidered scarlet cloth), vestment purchased at Church (RC) supply store on Lower East Side (NYC), and worn (June 8, 1966) by SADIE MASSEY, in her apt., BEACON HOTEL, NYC; in presence of LANE ANDERSON (*See DOOM*) and TOM JONES; with her bishop's cope Massey wore only a pair of high-heeled white shoes. Earlier Massey had lighted incense and candles and colored lights; she also played Ragas and Talas (World-Pacific 1431, side 2) on her Garrard turntable; Anderson, Jones, and Massey had consumed ⅓ oz. of marijuana and 1 gm. of hashish; for a time the three embraced sitting on the Castro-convertible sofa (*See PAPAGENO.*) Then Anderson and Jones removed their clothing and opened the Castro-convertible sofa. Massey retained her bishop's cope but kicked off her white shoes before lying down on the sofa. While Jones and Massey kissed and embraced, Anderson performed cunnilingus on her (Massey). Then Anderson mounted Massey; she sighed softly when his member penetrated her; supina iacens laevum poplitem duplicare iubetur, dextro crure porrecto. Anderson in eam incumbit et membro inserto 45 ad amussim ictus infert. Then Massey supina iacere et crura attollere iubetur. Anderson crura eius sursum impellit quoad pedes illius iuxta mamas positi sint. Tum Jaspium caulem alte inserit quoad in Puellam penetret infantem:

While Jones *supinus iacet protentis cruribus* and Massey *illi varica insidet utroque crure in fronte protento.* By this time Jones had begun to entertain many confused feelings. When Anderson hoisted Massey's thighs over his waist and mounted her from behind, Jones remained an idle observer. He wondered if Anderson considered their orgy payment for having been cuckolded by Jones; Jones concluded that this was the case, for when Anderson placed Sadie Massey's ankles on his shoulders and began fucking her with deep lunging thrusts, Jones felt extremely uncomfortable. Massey's sensual groans redoubled his discomfort. (*See DOOM and PAPAGENO.*)

BLACK RESIGNS, as played by Thomas Bahr against TOM JONES (Aug. 3, 1966) at the Old Colony Bar in Ptn., Mass.; Jones had played a queen's Gambit opening and Bahr had replied with the Gruenfeld Defense. White continued to mount pressure and launched a mating attack on the kingside. The resignation came on the 26th move after white had won a piece and had a decisive positional advantage. After black's 22nd move:

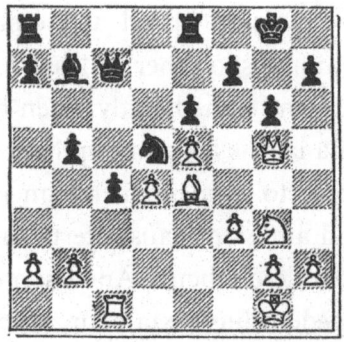

WHITE	BLACK
23 N-R5	Q-K2
24 N-B6 ck	NxN
25 PxN	Q-B1
26 BxB	Resigns

BOAT HOUSE, property of OSWALD KLUTZ in Ptn., Mass.; site of illicit rendezvous (Aug. 5, 1966) between MARJORIE FALIS and RUDI TREYF; Falis and Treyf had left the Klutz' cocktail party separately to avoid detection. Although this was the third such encounter between them, Marjorie Falis felt extreme anxiety. "My husband would kill me," she said, as Treyf held her in a tight embrace on the floor of the boat house. "He's not so tough," replied Rudi Treyf, "I saw him take it on the chin the other night at the A (Atlantic) House (Ptn.) The waiter laid him flat for his big mouth." As Marjorie Falis protested that her husband would use a knife or a gun, "if he got mad enough," Rudi Treyf removed her L.L. Bean's dungarees and proceeded to have intercourse with her. Falis felt diminishing pleasure until her only concernwas that her husband would discover them in the boat house. When Treyf had finished having intercourse with her, he said, "You're too tense, Marjorie. You should loosen up. We'll have more fun the second time around." Falis said, "Fuck off, Rudi."

BOX OF KLEENEX TISSUES (LARGE), attacked (morning, June 4, 1966) by TIFFANY and three of her kittens at SADIE MASSEY's apt., BEACON HOTEL, NYC; the disturbance made by the cats awoke Massey and TOM JONES, who had sublet his apt. (*See CROCHET WORK*) for June and July and moved to the

Beacon Hotel. She said, "O Tom, love, please take the tissues away from the cats. I can't get up." Tom Jones got out of bed and carried the box of Kleenex tissues out of reach of the cats. Sadie Massey said, "O, love, you're so wonderful." Tom Jones replied, "Well, let's get rid of the kittens and go up to Provincetown for the summer." (*See STREET SINGER, and DICED CHICKEN WITH ALMONDS.*) Sadie Massey protested, "But they won't be old enough for another week." Tom Jones said, "O.K., let's go back to sleep. It's only four-thirty." Sadie Massey said, "I won't be able to sleep now. Do you want some grass?"

BRICK, upon which rested a red glass water pipe which was smoked (June 16, 1965) in turn by Paco Funes, LARRY EARLY, and TOM JONES in the Funes home on River St., Hbkn., N.J.; Early remarked he had at that moment remembered a sad but funny experience; he related that he had once accompanied a friend to the post office in Rockefeller Plaza (NYC) upon the completion of the friend's massive novel, 7 years in progress. (Early called this "the best Marxist fiction I ever saw.") The ms. was in a manila envelope addressed to a publisher in England. Before the author's eyes a careless clerk ran the bulky package through a large stamping machine which tore it up into thousands of pieces. Early said, "The poor bastard was so broke he didn't have money to have a copy made. It took him 5 years to paste it back together." (*See CHEMICAL FIBER.*)

BROTHER OF THE LEFT-HAND PATH, expression borrowed at second hand from Western Occultism by TOM JONES and employed by him to describe persons whom he didn't like. Usage confined mainly to years as undergraduate at Columbia Univ. (1957–1961). PETER FRITZ would give in response, "Brother of the Left-Hand Path, Probationer, Practicus, Philosphicus, perhaps even Dominus Liminis, Adeptus Within and Without Major, and Exemptus, but never alas, Ipsissimus."

BRUTALS, THE, rock 'n' roll group appearing in the Atlantic House (Ptn., Mass.) nightly on the weekends during 1966 summer season; TOM JONES and SADIE MASSEY attended performance (July 7, 1966) and heard The Brutals sing their popular "Saigon Baby"; lyrics follow:

> She's my Saigon baby / And she's only 17 / She was my buddy's before me / Until he split the scene / She's the best piece I've had since I left Japan / And her little lemon-squeezer can really please a man / . . . One night when she was walking / With her girlfriend in the street / Some GI's grabbed them, held them / Down in a back seat / When they were through, they'd / Really blown her mind / And now she stays happy / With any GI she can find. (repeat)

Jones sipped a Carling Black Label beer while The Brutals were on stage and Massey danced with a tall, blond boy wearing a mustache and steel-rim glasses. When she returned to the table Massey said, "Wow, The Brutals are out of sight!" Jones agreed they were.

BUCKWHEAT BREAD, baked with buckwheat flour by Hilda Funes and served (Aug. 27, 1965) to her guests TOM JONES and LANE ANDERSON, in Hbkn., N.J.; with the bread Hilda Funes served tea in glasses. Paco Funes rolled several fat marijuana cigarettes laced with hashish. Lane Anderson complained that the bread was too hard for him to chew. He said he had a pathological fear of the dentist and had only been once in his life. Jones told Funes an anecdote about a girl they knew in common that JERRY DENFIELD had told JACOB LOWE earlier in the morning. Hilda Funes and Anderson chatted about VALERIE ANDERSON's recent cold. Jones and Anderson bought $40 worth of hashish from Paco Funes, who had received some that day from a Lebanese merchant seaman.

BURNT PIECE OF DRIFTWOOD, sat upon (Sept. 17, 1966) by TOM JONES as he gazed across the bay at Truro, in Ptn., Mass.; Jones considered that, as an American, he could have no means of useful political action. He felt very strongly that only those born in China could eventually hope to realize themselves through political participation, and then only because politics had become "thoroughly integrated into the life-style." (Jones) For him there remained two ways: deliberate cultivation of an acid (LSD-25)-oriented schizophrenia, or art. He had felt always lonely when, strongly committed to his poetry, he would spend months of self-exile from society. Often he felt the joys of writing were too few. A new way of life, a way of staying high and honorably getting by with help from his friends, began to tug at him with a deep appeal. Jones said, "If I don't mind going crazy, I might as well be already." His experiences with drugs had been the most startling in his life. (*See WHY IS EVERYONE SO CRAZY? and CIGARETTE ASH.*)

C

CADILLAC BEEF LIVER FOR DOGS, two cans of which were picked from the shelf (June 8, 1966) of an all-night grocery store on the corner of 74th St. & Columbus Ave., N.Y.C., by TOM JONES; Jones was shopping for SADIE MASSEY who told him that the cats preferred this brand of dog food to all brands of cat food. The proprietor of the store, a Puerto Rican, told Jones: "You know, they make this stuff for spades? It's cheap food, man, they just heat it up in the can. I sell it to them right here. And I've known some of them for years, they don't own no dog or nothin'. You know I seen one of 'em sittin' on his stoop once eatin' it cold out of the can with a spoon. They're just like animals. You Americans should stop trying to civilize 'em and get 'em back to work. Us (sic) Whites oughta hang together."

CANTHARIDES (*C. vesicatoria*), given (July 10, 1966) to TOM JONES by LAURENCE FAST as Jones and SADIE MASSEY were leaving the Cellar Bar in Ptn., Mass.; Fast said, "She's a groovy chick, man. Here, put some of this in your orange juice tomorrow morning."

CHEMICAL FIBER, described (June 7, 1965) by TOM JONES as the subject of an industrial film he had seen; Jones said the fiber was spun out of a tube to create a substitute for the conventional mattress and bed. Jones was speaking to Paco Funes and LARRY EARLY in the ANDERSON living room, Hbkn., N.J. Funes looked forward to the day when such "instant" beds could be created by portable, inexpensive "tubes, like fire extinguishers." (Funes) Early said he imagined the near future would provide to the consumer all manner of "instant ready-mades" (Early), including houses and cars and airplanes. Early said he had a fantasy of going to a deserted meadow and following simple instructions "on a giant shaving can type of thing with nozzles and dials" (Early), to produce a completed house within minutes. Jones said, "Such a house ought to be constructed in such a way that it would disappear when you weren't in it." Jones, Funes, and Early continued to smoke marijuana and wait for LANE ANDERSON to return in order to drive them into NYC. (*See BRICK.*)

CHICKEN'S TONGUE (From the Chinese, ch'u-chien), used to describe her clitoris (Aug. 18, 1966), by ALICE FAITH to TOM JONES in Ptn., Mass.; in her directive, "Kiss my chicken's tongue"; after Jones had performed cunnilingus on Faith, she told him that "chicken's tongue" was the term used in classical Chinese eroticism to describe the clitoris. Faith told Jones that her information on the subject came from the volume *Sexual Life in Ancient China*, by R. H. Van Gulik, which had been given to her by a NYC publisher. (*See FIXER, THE.*)

CHILDREN'S WEEK, a week so designated by the HOBOKEN PARENTS FOR PEACE in which the children drew crayon pictures of the U.S. flag in an inverted position to dramatize a "condition of national emergency." (*U.S. Flag Manual*) This week was observed Oct. 10–17, 1959, but was not continued in any succeeding year.

CIGARETTE ASH, brushed from the lap of TOM JONES (Aug. 15, 1966) in the home of BLACKY FALIS in Ptn., Mass.; the ash fell to the carpet where Jones's foot ground it into the fabric as he continued speaking: "I'm convinced that grass and acid, used over a very short period, tend to induce schizophrenia. But I would prefer to entirely do without such terminology. It simply no longer seems appropriate. There is a growing segment of the best young people in this country which is deliberately driving itself crazy, which insists on the absolute integrity of being crazy as a way of life, and seeks certain transcendental experiences through drug-oriented madness." Falis in reply said, "That's pot psychosis. And it's not new. Madness should not be romanticized. The terrible feelings of being squeezed out of yourself, the fragmentation, the obsessive inner voices, impulses, shapes, all running amok inside your head. This is what madness is about. Fuck the rest." Jones said, "I think you're wrong, Blacky. I feel deep inside of me that what you describe can be potentially liberating, a kind of renewal. But there are all kinds of ways of going crazy." (*See BURNT PIECE OF DRIFTWOOD and WHY IS EVERYONE SO CRAZY?*)

COMING DOWN ON ME, expression used by TOM JONES in conversation with SADIE MASSEY in the Cellar Bar (July 9, 1966), Ptn., Mass.; Jones related that earlier in the day he had been roughly treated in conversation with LAURENCE FAST over the subject of white racial hatred. Jones said, "He was really coming down on me about race, saying things like, 'What do you know White-boy about being Black? You come on so hip, but what do you really know about anything?' I told him, 'Dig it, I don't know *any* spades as well as you do. That's nowhere.'" Massey said she had never encountered that sort of treatment from Fast. She wondered what Jones had done to deserve it.

CONTROL YOUR DOWNS, advice given by ALICE FAITH (Sept. 15, 1966) to PETER PONZINI on his expression of interest in putting aside his "lethargy" (Ponzini) with the use of "speed" = methadrine (Faith); at Ponzini's house on Shankpntr. Rd., Ptn., Mass. She told him it was important to make a list of "things-to-do" (Faith) each day and accomplish every item on the list. She said the list of tasks should be adapted specifically to suit Ponzini's ambitions and interests. "They don't have to be big things," said Faith. She added, "You have to keep your balance. The important thing is to control your downs so that you can get things done. It's smart to make a shooting schedule and stick to it." Faith admitted that she herself was unable to adhere to such a regimen, but recognized that she had a weak character: "I can't help cheating when it comes to drugs." (Faith) (*See AKTEDRON*.)

COOPER, EDGAR (1924–), Am. writer; son of a wealthy merchant who owned factories in Oswego, N.Y.; spent 4 years in U.S. Navy after being graduated from Princeton Univ., B.A. (1945); set about literary career as critic and short-story writer. Became associate editor of IMPARTIAL REVIEW, 1952. His books include *Belligerence* (criticism) and *Painful Revels* (stories). Friendships with BLACKY FALIS and EUGENE ANGRIE. (*See SQUASH*.)

COPPER MANDALA (ON CHAIN), worn around the neck of SADIE MASSEY (April 27, 1966) as she sat before her Veena (Hindi & Sanskrit-Indian lyre) in her apt. in the BEACON HOTEL, NYC; TOM JONES sat cross-legged in front of her smoking a water pipe filled with marijuana and hashish. Massey strummed the Veena softly and said, "You know, I was hypnotized once by somebody who put me into a trance by making me concentrate on a medal he held in front of him on a long chain. There were other people there. When I was in a deep trance he held a match to his own finger and I felt the fire burning me. When he pricked his arm with a needle, I felt it. He put a sugar cube in his mouth and my mouth tasted sweet." Jones said, "Wow, that's incredible."

CROCHET WORK, in the form of a handbag, made (May 28, 1966) in the Cedar Bar, NYC, by Mary Halter; Halter had phoned Jones in response to his sublet ad in the *NY Times;* she told him he would recognize her as the girl who crocheted. When Jones arrived at the Cedar Bar he found Mary Halter at a table surrounded by four men. Ignoring her suggestion that "everyone" go to look at the apt., Jones escorted Halter out of the bar and into a taxicab. On the drive uptown, as Jones discussed leaving certain valuables in the apt., Halter replied that it was all right with her if Jones "checked up from time to time to see that everything is the way you like it."

CURLY BLACK HAIR (PUBIC), discovered (Sept. 10, 1966) by TOM JONES; adhering to a bar of soap in his bathroom, at his residence 606 Comml. St., Ptn., Mass. Jones believed the hair belonged to SADIE MASSEY, who had just left the country with BLACKY FALIS; sight of the hair caused Jones great remorse. (*See DUNES, ROACH, SHE SAID SHE SAID, and TIFFANY.*)

CZECHOSLOVAKIAN MACHINE GUNS, referred to (July 27, 1965) in conversation by Paco Funes with LANE ANDERSON, in the Funes residence, River St., Hbkn., N.J.; Funes related an incident which occurred several years previous while he was a resident in East Harlem, NYC. He said his premises had been under police surveillance, which determined him to get rid of 4 Czechoslovakian machine guns he was keeping for Honduran revolutionaries. When the police entered his apt. they confiscated only a small quantity of cocaine. Funes remarked he had been fortunate to remove the "stuff." (Funes) Anderson commented, "It was wise for another reason, Paco. Iron, all of itself, works on a man and attracts him. Those are Odysseus's words to his son." (Bk. xix, line 13) Funes appeared to receive these words as insulting. He said, "Wow, Man, you see everything in terms of a book. Like it all happened a long time ago and you've solved it. It's true, isn't it? Like if Xenophon had died fighting for the Persians, what would we *really* know about Socrates?"

D

DAMAGED UPHOLSTERY, in the Circle Bar, Wash. St., Hbkn., N.J., ignored (Aug. 4, 1965) by TOM JONES who sat on an exposed spring across from JACOB LOWE in a corner booth; Jones was eager for the opportunity to converse with Lowe, whom he greatly admired. As they sipped beer, Jones brought up the novels of BLACKY FALIS. Lowe remarked, "Falis is a talented boor. A vulgarian. Unfortunately he has assumed leadership in the movement of Shit that he used to warn of. I see no hope for him." (See *SALMON-PINK TABLECLOTH*.) The subject of conversation shifted to politics and Jones listened attentively as Lowe expatiated on the incompetence of America's leaders to deal with situations.

DAWN AT A HBKN. BALLFIELD, 5TH & RIVER STS., title of a poem written by LANE ANDERSON (Sept. 6, 1965); Anderson apologized to his wife, VALERIE, for failing their plan of an evening's entertainment in NYC, and excused himself to TOM JONES for "hanging him up." (See *PURPLE DRESS*.) Anderson explained that he had stopped off on his way home at the Cellar Bar (Hbkn.) intending to have only one drink. However, he had lost track of the hour and his condition. Finding himself "inebriated," Anderson described how he had determined to take a sobering walk in the cold night rain, ending up at the Hbkn. ballfield where he wrote a poem.

DEANER 100

He presented ms. of the poem (text follows below) to his wife, and conceded he had been so pleased with it that he had continued to drink at HELGA'S HIDEAWAY instead of returning home. Text of poem:

> The fall wind is sweeping even the running
> lights of the ferryboats before it, little
> wonder the wet leaves scoot too across
> this turf,—How foolish my day's routines are,
> before this grave!—the white H of the goalposts
> looms out through the rain, the backstop
> drips noisily—there are Mr. G., and Mr. B.,
> and Mr. M., they are my teachers, coaches,
> who cry encouragement to a still-believing
> boy, they guide him through the afternoons,
> he is leaping out of bed in the blue dawns,
> oh the misery is sweeping over me now,
> the cold flies like bullets into every pore,
> the fall wind is sweeping even the running
> lights of the ferryboats before it, little
> wonder the wet leaves scoot too across
> this turf, this grave, this terrifying grave.

DEANER 100, a synthetic protein (2-Dimetilaminoetanol), recommended to BLACKY FALIS (July 15, 1966) in his motor launch in Ptn. Harbor (Mass.), by TOM JONES; Jones told Falis that this psychic energizer, remarked on by Huxley in *Brave New World Revisited*, and available through Riker Laboratories, Inc. (Northridge, Calif.) would allow him (Falis) to continue to smoke marijuana without suffering the debilitating lethargy and loss of memory that Falis had complained of, and which had caused him to give up the drug. Jones added that the natural protein of which Deaner was a synthetic was a protein found in human brain cells. Jones said, "It's like charging the battery." (*See RAT STUDIES.*)

DEAR DR. LORENZ,
    In a recent experiment I read of, laboratory rats were put into an environment with New York City air to breathe. They attacked each other recklessly, ensuing bloody chaos. Why is it the inhibitions against intra specific aggression so completely broke down? I am very curious to find out. Can you explain it to me?

Charles Falis (signed)

Above is complete text of letter written (May 20, 1966, 2 a.m.) in New York by CHARLES BLACKY FALIS. It was never posted and remains in the top lefthand drawer of his desk at 336 Central Park West.

DEAR TOM, O SPAIN IS SUPER-GROOVY! First sentence of letter received (Oct. 12, 1966) in Ptn., Mass., by TOM JONES. The letter was postmarked Barcelona, Spain (Oct. 5, 1966) and was signed by SADIE MASSEY. Text of letter follows:

    Rosas del Mar   3 October

    Dear Tom,
        O Spain is super-groovy! I am in this really paradisiacal little town with a pink beach and all the little houses are pink too. It is called Roses of the Sea in English.

Every morning I get up before eight and go swimming, O it's so lovely! Sometimes I just float along very quietly and listen to all the strange sounds. The voices from the shore sound like music. O Tom dear, I am so happy. If you could only see how happy I really am you wouldn't be angry with me anymore or look at me with those sad eyes of yours. No, Tom, you couldn't be cross with me because for the first time in my life I am beginning to understand some of the things that I have been reading about in Krishna Murti and I really feel at peace. Can you imagine? I haven't had anything to drink since I came here or anything to smoke either. I don't know if it's around, but I haven't even felt like it.

Blacky helped me to understand that all those things I thought I wanted with him were wrong for me. I mean being with him for those weeks really showed me where he's at. You were right about him but you didn't know it because you were being nasty and jealous. He's a very heavy cat but he's all mixed up in this silly game of proving himself in everything he does. And he's so hyped up! Really, Tom, he never relaxes, not for a minute. We split up in Barcelona last week.

O Darling Tom, I know this is going to be hard for you to understand. But I have nobody in the world I can talk to the way I can talk to you and I want so for you not to worry about me and think I'm just ruining my life on silly things and being irresponsible. But, Tom, I just know that if I can find the words to tell you about Carlos you'll be able to see that I'm really so happy and finding myself at last. Carlos is the first man I've ever met who really understands women. O Tom, I felt from the first moment I saw him that he was seeing deep, deep into me. You just know he knows. His brother is a duke, O but what a surprise! I always thought a duke was very severe and wore a monocle or else was some kind of drunk who brooded forever about the way things used to be and maybe had a romantic dueling scar or something. O but they're not like that at all. We went hunting quail on the estate—of course I didn't fire a shot—but their friends were there and they're all so intelligent and kind and courteous. Carlos most of all. He can make me feel like a woman down to the tips of my toes just by looking at me! Anyway, Tom dearest, we're together here at Rosas del Mar and everything is just so terrific. Some evenings we go into Barcelona, it's only an hour away, and have a lovely meal by candlelight and, O Tom, don't think I'm a romantic little slut I couldn't bear it. Please, Tom, see that I'm happy. And please try, try, try to understand.

Always be my friend—I hope this letter reaches you,

S. (signed)

DELUX KOSS PRO-4 STEREO HEADPHONES, referred to by SADIE MASSEY in her sentence to TOM JONES, "These are a groove. I wouldn't have it any other way." (May, 1966, NYC) Massey owned five sets of earphones which were used by her friends to listen to stereo records. The earphones were advertised as adding a "new dimension to listening pleasure," by locking out external noise and allowing full-range sound "over the entire audio spectrum." Sadie Massey told Jones, "Not only can you hear better than you ever imagined possible, but if you want to talk you can just take off the earphones. You don't have to talk over the sound." She added that a Swedish electronics engineer she had picked up in the East Village (NYC) had installed the earphones for her.

DENFIELD, JERRY (1933–), Am. playwright, director, and actor; b. in N. Dakota, father was minor-league baseball player; grew up in W. Dakota Badlands; little formal education; ran away from home at 16 yrs., and held assorted odd jobs until arriving in NYC (1952). There he came under the influence of JACOB LOWE, and met LANE ANDERSON and LARRY EARLY. Denfield's work in off-Broadway productions (*A Rotten Plum*, 1955; *The Boys on Christopher St.*, 1957); as a performer and director drew early comment. His best-known plays are *Ma's Funeral* (1956), and *Your Father's Moustache* (1963). As as important member of the bohemian living community headed by Lowe in Hbkn., N.J., Denfield was known for his eccentric appearance and brooding temperament. (*See FORTY-THREE CARDBOARD BOXES.*)

DIALOGUE CONCERNING THE GREAT WRITER (June 21, 1965), extended colloquy betw. LANE ANDERSON and TOM JONES concerning JACOB LOWE in Hbkn., N.J., at the Anderson residence and such establishments as The Triangle Bar, HELGA'S HIDEAWAY, and #11 River St.; Anderson related how he had taken an apt. on Mott St. (NYC) upon graduating from Yale (1952) in search of poetic experience and youthful love affairs. The life he encountered, "a sordid life," Anderson explained, was on the outer fringes of the Greenwich Village social and literary circles. He told of his first encounter with Lowe, then largely unknown, in the San Remo Bar. Lowe was sitting at a corner table with one arm around a hysterical woman and the other sexually frisking a young man. Eventually, Anderson was drawn into conversation with the young man, who introduced him to Jacob Lowe. In a short time he was undergoing group therapy with several contemporaries (JERRY DENFIELD, LARRY EARLY) under Lowe's guidance. During the course of the analytic process the two men shared an intimate relationship. Anderson trusted Lowe's advice in most of his actions and came to view him as a great teacher. "Later," Anderson said, "when I married Sylvia, my first wife, Jacob (Lowe) told me, 'You're on your own now.' He thought I deserted him for a woman. After that he always made sex a big deal." Nevertheless, as their personal contact diminished, he continued to esteem Lowe for his magnificent purpose and stirring prose style. He also praised Lowe's willingness to assist younger writers to achieve self-confidence ("in his arms, as it were," Anderson) and his absolute integrity. Tom Jones saw a pattern in the man's gruff, erratic exterior and his uneven, idiosyncratic prose style. He believed that Lowe was a gifted man who had squandered his talents in too many places, but who was also a generous man and a formidable intellect. Anderson spiced the topic by saying, "He's (Lowe) really fantastically mad. Crazy as a loon. I bet he hears voices. He thinks all dentists are oral sadists and has all kinds of queer superstitions." And he added, "But he's (Lowe) so clever that he can make a scheme to fit anything. If you led him around writing down his advice on how to improve things here and there, he'd be able to tell you how to go about it. And he'd be right. Jacob (Lowe) is always right." Tom Jones declared he was unable to see how this could be so, as Anderson conceded that Lowe was also prudish, a liar, unfair to his friends, and a poor husband. Anderson argued that such ad hominem and "Physician Heal Thyself" (Anderson) arguments could bear no weight. Jones was made to agree, "I guess if Jacob (Lowe) really wanted to help someone, he could." (*See ROUND TABLE.*)

DICED CHICKEN WITH ALMONDS AND CHINESE VEGETABLES, an order of which was served (May 26, 1966) to TOM JONES and SADIE MASSEY at the Good Earth Restaurant on 72nd St. in NYC. Jones and Massey dined together after spending the afternoon in Massey's apt. smoking marijuana, watching a sports program on the television, and having sexual intercourse. Later they showered and went to a neighborhood movie house where they saw *The Chase* and *The Collector,* neither of which they enjoyed. In bed together that night, they discussed their desire to go away from the city and spend the summer in Ptn., Mass. (*See BOX OF KLEENEX and STREET SINGER.*)

DON'T MAKE FUN OF THE SWAMI, statement addressed in anger (June 12, 1966) to TOM JONES by SADIE MASSEY at the BEACON HOTEL, NYC; in the evening Massey had accompanied her grandparents to a benefit dinner for the Anti-

Defamation League of B'nai B'rith, at which Sammy Davis, Jr., was the guest speaker. Jones had occupied his time alone by constructing an obscene collage which employed photographs from various magazines and three 2" x 3" snapshots of Swami Satchidananda. Jones replied, "Don't bitch at me. I'm working off my hard-sin karma."

DOOM, term used by TOM JONES to describe the Andersons (June 8, 1966) prior to LANE ANDERSON's visit to Jones and SADIE MASSEY, at BEACON HOTEL, NYC; visit was 1st reunion betw. Anderson and Jones since discovery of Jones as VALERIE ANDERSON's lover. (*See THREE BOILED POTATOES*); Jones encountered Anderson in Greenwich Village (NYC) bar and felt obligated by Anderson's affable behavior to extend an invitation; Jones told Massey, re Andersons, "I can't imagine what we have in common anymore. They were sort of groovy when it was 'in' to be doomed. He was always brooding over the bomb and his graduate-school education, and she was always reading Kierkegaard, or someone like that. You know, they were very down all the time unless they got loaded on booze, then they might do something crazy, like smash up the car or have an affair." (Jones) (*See BISHOP'S COPE and PAPAGENO.*)

DOPE KIDS ARE RUINING PROVINCETOWN, remark by OSWALD KLUTZ (July 14, 1966) to Hyman Hyman, RUDI TREYF, TOM JONES, SADIE MASSEY) and Catherine Petú Klutz in his home in Ptn., Mass.; Jones insisted that as a patron of modern artists, he (Klutz) ought to take a more sympathetic outlook on change of all kinds. Rudi Treyf said that he knew the conventional forms of painting and writing would not be extended a hundred years. He suggested that Klutz knew this too, and saw the youthful hippies as precursors of generations who would utterly devalue his collection of contemporary art. Tom Jones ventured in agreement, "Art performed and experienced in a drug-oriented culture, say in one hundred years from now, will look back on our avant-garde with the same curiosity with which we look at the paintings of schizophrenics." (*See HELLO TO YOU.*)

DOPPELGÄNGER (wraith-like double), term used (March, 1965) by HENRY JONES, in conversation with his son, TOM; father and son discussed problems of faith, in last important talk held between them, at the Jones family residence, 410 West End Ave., NYC; T. Jones said, "As a Jew in a secular century, I feel I have escaped my religion. The Diaspora is at an end. My people have outlived their curse. There is no great racial fear to bind my allegiance." Henry Jones protested that the consequences of such a position would lead in later life to haunting uncertainty. The Doppelgänger, he said, would inhabit his son's life and cause him misery, unable to find in the culture what he had given up by birth: ". . . the strong sense of continuity of a people, a real heritage and tradition." Tom Jones said his father would be surprised in confronting the hostile attitude of the Sabras (born in Israel) toward NYC Jewry. He said, "These people have contempt for donations to a cause they risk their lives in every day. Besides, what kind of Jews are we, with a name like Jones?" Henry Jones told his son, "My son, the name you bear is one of pride in the Jewish tradition. As late as the '56 fighting we Joneses, in the person of Speedy Jones, who owned oil and Texas cattle, was one of the most decorated heroes in the Israeli army. Your grandfather Jones, who owned several factories in the Passaic area, was an outstanding man in the community and a fine merchant. The name stretches as far back as the Maccabees. Tom, Einstein, Freud, and Marx, were all our people. To abandon your tradition is nothing to be taken lightly. These men were all modern in their thinking, but they remained Jews. And that's because once you're born a Jew, you die a Jew. You can't suddenly cease being a Jew, even if you change your name from Finkelstein to Fink. No sir, you might as well accept it and stop hanging around all that goyim cunt." (H. Jones)

DRAFT-DODGER RAPES VIET HERO'S WIDOW—AND THEN BEHEADS HER, headline banner for *Hush*, a weekly scandal-atrocity newspaper, purchased (April, 1966) by TOM JONES, who was unable to walk away from the newsstand where he saw the headline displayed. He read the lead story walking to meet SADIE MASSEY at a nearby Schrafft's restaurant. He discovered that the draft-dodger referred to was a refugee from the Kaiser's Germany, living in Paris during the late 1920s. The Viet-hero of the headline was a mercenary fighting in Indo-China for the French. He had deserted his wife five years earlier and she was employed at the time of her death as an exotic dancer in a Paris nightclub. The killer confessed to the crime, claiming that he had sought treatment in a Paris mental hospital, but had been turned away. Tom Jones gave the newspaper to Sadie Massey, who left it in the ladies·

room at Schrafft's.

DUNES OF NORTH TRURO (MASS., USA), where BLACKY FALIS took SADIE MASSEY for a ride in a rented beach jeep (Aug. 22, 1966). They encountered a windstorm on the dunes. Massey said, "It's wild out here." Falis said the continual turbulence was linked to the sun's energy. Falis stopped driving the car and embraced Massey. He said, "It sounds strange for me, but I surprise myself. I believe we're actually going to go away together, but each time it hits me I think something's bound to fuck up: Marjorie will slash her wrists, someone will get sick, Johnson will push the button, something." Massey replied that even if there were a third world war she knew "There would be a lot of love before the end." Falis replied abruptly, "Fuck you, it would be a horror show." Massey said that when the atmosphere became deadly to all human life, "There would be immense compassion vibrations. The light and the dark. Like a trip." Falis replied, "If that's what it does to your head, I don't want to take any."

DUNHILL PIPE STEM (EBONY), bitten through (March 18, 1965) by JACOB LOWE at 306 Washington St., Hbkn., N.J.; Lowe was seated in ANDERSON living room in the company of LANE ANDERSON and TOM JONES, discussing the nature of political behavior; Lowe withdrew the broken pipe stem from his mouth and said, "Years ago a professor of mine at the University of Chicago told me to smoke a pipe and clamp down hard when people said impossible things to me." "I insist, Jacob," said Tom Jones, "even if you think I'm being impossible. A lot of the organized activities you champion seem as remote from reality as the smug academicians who say, 'Politics has no place here,' or those who come on with, 'If you protest the war, you'll be helping the enemy.' The people you are trying to reach, the young people, are convinced that political demonstrations accomplish nothing. You gave us good ideas for utopian living communities, but even these will only come about after groups of individuals have *individually* resolved to leave the culture completely." Jacob Lowe nodded his head sententiously. "Look, Tom, my faith in young people, and hence in meaningful political action, is based on the expectation for change that you don't have. These kids get angry at what their parents have left for them and are excited enough to make plans and organize to change things. SDS, the Berkeley kids, the civil rights kids, the kids who burn their draft cards, SNCC, all of them are changing things by their very presence on the scene. You may not perceive the changes dramatically, or even think they're real, but I've been around long enough to know they are." "But, Jacob," Lane Anderson began impatiently, "these activities are only peripheral. They are tokens of the worsening position. As things get further along the way toward total annihilation, the protest movements get louder, too. You know I've agreed with you for years, but with the assassination, and Vietnam, the whole technological-cybernetic horror, I mean the feeling you get about America is so fucking desperate. All of the kicky people being pointlessly kicky, the LSD thing, all that comes from deep hopelessness. What Tom says is a reflection of that, even if he won't admit it." "Not so, not so," Tom Jones interjected. "Both of you are out of touch. Look, *emotionally* the young *are* committed. But we've learned that politics, by its nature, always shits on freedom and the arts. That's the way it's got to be. The Young Left or the New Left or whatever are just remnants of a politics that is going out. The real new force is the cyberneticists, and these people are the most frightening of all, the real Frankensteins." Jacob Lowe listened patiently to what Lane Anderson and Tom Jones were saying. Then he said, "In all of what you've said, the two of you, you've been confusing the human side of the problem with some kind of abstract notion of what politics is like. This is very common today. But until you and others, who *do* care, can see all political interests in terms of human solutions to the general dilemma, we'll always wind up like this. Nowhere." Lane Anderson munched on a stale English tea biscuit. (*See* BEETHOVEN.)

DYSTROPHES, LES, title of film by Lynn Ratener, screened (Aug. 26, 1965) at the Bridge Theater, NYC; screening attended by LANE ANDERSON and TOM JONES: film depicted the naked bodies of muscular dystrophy patients in a variety of grotesque tableaux. Lane Anderson complained hours later in the San Remo Bar, NYC, that during his viewing of the film he had experienced physical nausea and goose pimples. He doubted, however, that the film was a work of art. Tom Jones advised Anderson to forget about such considerations altogether; he suggested that the New Aesthetics would be highly indebted to cybernetics, and operate between the biophysical response and intellectual cognition. Jones said he was certain a type of art would soon appear for which it would be requisite for the audience to take a prescribed dosage of a prescribed drug. Anderson said he was bewildered by what Jones frequently said to him. "You've changed a hell of a lot since we met, ol' buddy" (Anderson).

E

EARLY, LARRY (1932–), Am. painter; b. Rochester, N.Y., parents were dance instructors at local ballroom; after 4 yrs. in USAF, stationed in Spain, Early returned to NYC and enrolled at N.Y.U.; B.A. (1957); for his livelihood Early taught at succession of secondary schools in N.J. and NYC, but disturbed the administration at each institution with his pro-Peking politics. At other times Early has worked as a house painter and collection agent. He moved to Hbkn., N.J. (1959) with his wife (Ellen) and two children, hoping to live more cheaply there than in NYC; imp. member of bohemian living community, though violently opposed to liberal-utopian (nonactivist) political views of JACOB LOWE. Early's paintings, never popular, demonstrate a concern with texture leading to crudities of color and design, but informed with a passionate dialectical intensity. Characteristically, there are no human figures in Early's paintings.

ELECTROENCEPHALOGRAMS OF YOGIS, cited in conversation (May 8, 1966) by SADIE MASSEY, in NYC; in conversation with TOM JONES; Massey argued that exploration in the regions of precognition, intuition, and telepathy would open up dimensions of consciousness previously unknown to classical psychology. She supported her assumptions by pointing out that electroencephalograms of yogis in a state of *samadhi* show curves which do not correspond to any cerebral activities known in waking or sleep. (*See COPPER MANDALA.*)

ELEVEN WEST HUDSON ST., address in NYC where TOM JONES and SADIE MASSEY (wearing only body paint) attended (June 13, 1966) a party given in honor of Shrieko Cosey, the painter; a tall, young Englishman silently inserted his finger between Massey's buttocks, but Massey gave no sign of what was being done to her and Jones turned to overhear a conversation in which a big, unshaven man told a small, untidy man, "I used to think *The Recognitions* was the best in English since *Ulysses*." At a later point in the evening, a girl who said her eyes were on fire, jumped four stories to the street. (*See TOILET CHAIN.*)

ESPALIER (GREEN VINE), growing at 606 Comml. St., Ptn., Mass.; remarked upon by SADIE MASSEY (June 26, 1966) as she and TOM JONES arrived in Ptn. from NYC. Jones said, "Yeah, it's great here. Smell the sea." He carried their bags from the cab which had driven them from the airport.

EXPOSED PENIS, seen by TOM JONES as he sat with SADIE MASSEY (May 17, 1966) in the New Amsterdam Movie Theater on 42nd St., in NYC; the man sitting next to Jones had exposed himself by raising his raincoat over his hips; Jones discovered that the man wore no pants or socks, but had painted his legs from the ankle to the thigh with black shoe polish. Jones did not notice that the man sitting on the other side of Sadie Massey was carrying out a brusque maneuver under her (Massey's) clothing with an 8½" rubber dildo. Jones believed that the spasmodic pressure which Massey applied to his arm was due to her excitement over *Count Dracula's Guest,* which was nearing its climax.

F

FAITH, ALICE (1938–) , Am. nurse; discharged from St. Vincent's Hospital, NYC, on charges of drug theft and conduct unbecoming a registered nurse; filed suit (1963) on grounds of libel, slander, defamation of character, malicious mischief, and false arrest; awarded lifetime support by the State Supreme Court. Addicted to morphine, dexadrine, and Demerol, Faith dissipated herself as she drifted from one bohemian enclave to the next. Finding herself in a N.W. (U.S.) ski resort (spring, 1966) Faith decided to remain in America and spend the summer on Cape Cod (Mass.).

FALIS, CHARLES (BLACKY) (1924–), Am. writer; b., educated in NYC; parents were poor and money scarce in author's childhood. Attended The New School for Social Research and Harvard Univ., no degree. Published 1st novel, *The Palace of Pudend*, when only 23. It became immed. best seller and established Falis's reputation as one of Am.'s most discussed novelists. Later books are *When the Panting Stops* (1950), *The Armpit Freak* (1957), *Brute Blood* (1961), and *Crashed in the White House* (1965). Eliot Barnstone in the *Sat. Review* (Feb., 1965) called Falis "the only living writer in America who has a unified world view." Falis has demonstrated a relentless tenacity in tracing the pathological elements, often sexual, in contemp. Am. society. Falis bought house (1959) on Shankpntr. Rd., Ptn., Mass., since when he has divided his time between Cape Cod and NYC. Married (1951) to Hildegaard Innis, and again in 1965, to Marjorie Steinfeldt. (*See FALIS, MARJORIE STEINFELDT.*) At end of summer, 1966, Falis left his wife and traveled to Europe with SADIE MASSEY.

FALIS, MARJORIE STEINFELDT (1937–), 2nd wife of CHARLES "BLACKY" FALIS; b. of Jewish parents in NYC; she attended the Fieldston School and Barnard College, where she was graduated (B.A., 1959). Her chief interests were modern theater, current fashions, aquatic sports, and travel. She was employed at Hill & Wang, the publishers, when she met Falis in 1964. They were married the following year in NYC. Their first child, a boy, was born the same year.

FAST, LAURENCE (1933–), Am. Negro entertainer; grew up in Harlem (NYC); no secondary-school education; earned livelihood from age 14 as pimp, male prostitute, and drug peddler; began career as entertainer in Harlem nightclubs and at the Apollo Theater; later worked in Greenwich Village supper clubs and in Ptn., Mass.; known professionally as the "Ace of Spades." Friendship with BLACKY FALIS dating from late 1950s, when they met at a party in Harlem. Member of Black Muslim sect known as the Assassins (Arabic = under the influence of hashish). Fast told Falis that the sect was "late shit, man," punning on Shiite, a medieval religious order from which the Assassins developed. A recording of Fast's has been released with the title, "Wake Up, Whitey!" (*See MOISTENING PUDEND.*)

FIRE EXTINGUISHER

FIFTH DRINK, A, taken by BLACKY FALIS (Aug. 5, 1966) as he sat with TOM JONES in the Atlantic House Bar in Ptn., Mass.; Falis was drinking rye and soda and Jones had two Carling Black Label beers. As Falis ordered his fifth drink, Jones shook his head and continued with his sentence, "but aren't these kids still the vast minority?" Falis told Jones, "You'll see. There'll be changes. They're old enough to vote already." Jones disagreed, "Not for twenty years. These aren't the kids who enter politics. Several intermediary stages will happen before the whole thing synchronizes. Communal, psychedelic living centers, and then one of the smaller progressive states, perhaps New Mexico, will go over in government." Falis said, "No, no utopias here, Kid. What would be happening to the international suicide while America was getting wacked out on all these new drugs?" Jones replied, "Look, the other countries would be into drugs, too. I just think that since the psychedelic leadership is and will be white that America can point the way."

FIRE EXTINGUISHER, stolen in the morning (4 a.m.; June 19, 1965) from the Bartholomew Davis Preparatory School for Boys in Metuchen, N.J., by LANE ANDERSON, who had attended Davis as a boy, and TOM JONES; Anderson drove his 1948 Dodge to the deserted school gymnasium and Jones, following Anderson's instructions, ran into the building and removed the fire extinguisher. Later in the morning Anderson and Jones were chased on the highway by the state police (N.J.) after being warned off the premises of The Hillside Day School for Girls. The Hillside School and The Sunnybrook

School were competing in a lively game of lacrosse for the Upper Girls' Team Trophy. Anderson and Jones took refuge in the home of Lily Anderson, Lane Anderson's mother, who lived in Metuchen, N.J. Jones noticed that Mrs. Anderson had placed an open copy of Mary Baker Eddy's *Science and Health* on a table where it would receive the day's first light. Lane Anderson said, "Yeah, Mother's a Christian Scientist. She tried to bring us up that way. Once when I had a rash on my prick I prayed to Mary Baker Eddy for a health miracle, but it only got worse."

FIXER, THE, first-edition copy of the novel written by Bernard Malamud; published by Farrar Straus & Giroux, N.Y., 1966, 335 pp.; ALICE FAITH picked up book belonging to TOM JONES (Aug. 18, 1966), and asked, "Is this about junkies?" Tom Jones rolled over on his left side and stubbed out his cigarette in the ashtray on the night table. With his right hand he grabbed Alice Faith's pudend. He said, "No, it isn't. It's about a Jew. Let's fuck some more." Alice Faith pushed the book off the bed and it fell to the floor with a soft thud. (*See CHICKEN'S TONGUE.*)

FOLIAGE, New Eng. expression, used to describe regional woods (collectively) and their autumnal change in color; referred to by MARJORIE FAILS (Aug. 22, 1966) in her suggestion, "Let's take a walk in the woods, and watch the foliage, BLACKY." (addressed to her husband, in their bedroom, Ptn., Mass.); Marjorie Falis complained that her husband did not spend enough time with her, and said his many friends distracted him from herself and his work. Blacky Falis agreed to his wife's suggestion of a walk in the woods, and they drove to N. Truro (Mass.) and walked in a densely wooded area holding hands. Marjorie Falis told her husband that he did not "concentrate" (M. Falis) enough of his attention on her. She said she feared she did not involve enough of his energies. She blamed the hectic pace of their existence in Ptn. Blacky Falis reassured his wife by saying that the summer was nearly at an end and the swarm of people would soon depart. He said he had become "bogged down" (B. Falis) in his novel, and that this had distracted him from the important things around him. As he spoke to his wife, Falis was conscious of lying to her.

FORTY-THREE CARDBOARD BOXES, in the Hbkn. apt. of JERRY DENFIELD at 308 Wash. St., when visited by TOM JONES and LANE ANDERSON (Sept. 9, 1965). The boxes were filled with refuse that had accumulated over the past two years. Denfield preferred to keep the refuse in his apt. rather than carry it down to the street, five stories below. He would have preferred to dump it out of the courtyard window, but feared he would be seen and reported to the police. Consequently, Denfield became ashamed of the foul odor in his apt. and admitted very few of his friends. Because of his activities in the theater he kept irregular hours and seldom remained in Hbkn. for more than a few hours at a time. Anderson and Jones had glimpsed Denfeld through the adjacent courtyard window and walked upstairs to ask him to have a beer with them in the Circle Bar on Wash. St.

FOUL-SMELLING RAG, used by PETER KAZANOVSKY (May 7, 1965) at six in the morning, to wipe off the empty tables and bar in The Triangle Bar, Hbkn., N.J.; LANE ANDERSON and TOM JONES were Kazanovsky's first customers. He had not concluded wiping off the bar with the foul-smelling rag, thus he left it in front of Lane Anderson when he (Kazanovsky) went to shake the water out of two newly washed glasses and draw the beer. When he brought the beers to Anderson and Jones, Anderson said, "Christ, Petey, can you move this foul-smelling rag?" Kazanovsky replied in jest, "It's only beer, Lane." Anderson and Jones had spent the past 14 hrs. in bars in NYC's Greenwich Village. (*See LOOP OF HAIR.*)

FRITZ, PETER (1939–65), Am. graduate student and suicide; graduated from Columbia Univ. (B.A.); continued studies there in Eng. Lit.; suffered acute nervous anxiety much of the time. (*See KILLER.*) Friendship with TOM JONES. Response in *Village Voice* personals (*See I HAVE A GENIUS . . .*) led to relationship with TUKI LEE, who moved into Fritz's lodgings on the Lower East Side, NYC. This wanton union caused Fritz crushing remorse. He slashed his jugular vein and bled to death (Oct. 2, 1965) in Tompkins Square Park, NYC. (*See PETER'S FUNERAL and BROTHER OF THE LEFT-HAND PATH.*)

FUCKED IN THE ASS, quote taken from conversation (July 4, 1966) of BLACKY FALIS and OSWALD KLUTZ, in the Klutz summer home in Ptn., Mass. Falis's words were: "Fucked in the ass, that's what Johnson fears the most, that some other poisonous Texan with a strangled mind and a fat cock will ram it home." Falis, who was inebriated, had become an obvious embarrassment for Klutz, who nevertheless found it impossible to extricate himself. Several other guests at the Klutz's noisily prepared to leave, casting hesitant glances at Falis. Some said it was a "disgrace" to say such "vile things" about the President on Independence Day. Falis, who was enjoying himself immensely, grabbed hold of Klutz's shoulder and whispered in his ear: "The license a famous writer enjoys is quite astounding, isn't it?"

G

GENERAL ELECTRIC RANGE AND DISHWASHER, in her home in Ptn., Mass., on top of which MARJORIE FALIS sat (Aug. 4, 1966) talking to TOM JONES. Falis said, "I'm through taking psychedelics. It distorts your whole point of view. I'd rather smoke a little pot from time to time. Charles (Falis) has people here all the time. It's his scene. I mean I could never have people over here if I took acid or something." Jones said, "You could put a sign on the door saying Come Back Tomorrow."

GIMMIE, EDWARD (1932–), Am. businessman; founded the Psychedilly Botique Co., Inc., purveyor of curiosities to the users of psychedelic drugs; began career as door-to-door salesman of children's encyclopedias in Levittown, Pa., subject of article in *Business Today* (May, 1965) entitled "A New Horatio Alger?" in which Gimmie is quoted as saying, "If you want to sell the 'turned-on' set, you have to turn on with them. Of course, most of these people are creeps and commies, but does GM care who buys their products? These beatniks buy brand-name products all their lives." Gimmie met SADIE MASSEY (April 8, 1966), and had sexual intercourse with her that night, transmitting his pubic lice. (*See GLOM, ADOLF.*) TOM JONES said, "Sadie, for Christ's sake, why did you go to bed with that slob, Gimmie?" Sadie Massey replied,

"He is the strangest person I've ever met. He insisted I leave all my clothes on and just take off my panties." "Did you go through with it?" asked Tom Jones. "Don't be a masochist, darling," said Sadie Massey, "I shouldn't tell you anything." Tom Jones said, "You mean you would have given me his lousy crabs and not said a word?" "Well, I *did* tell you, didn't I?" replied Sadie Massey.

GLOM, ADOLF, DR. (1905–), Jewish-Am. physician; of German extraction, Glom was brought up and schooled in France; received medical degree from the Univ. of Paris, 1934; during the years 1937–44, Glom traveled in N. and N.W. Africa as an itinerant physician, amassing a large fortune through his treatment of syphilitic tribal chieftains. Payment was in ivory and gold. He is said to have been married several times in tribal ceremonies during this period. After exchanging his fortune for capital, he emigrated to the U.S. and became a citizen (1949). On Dec. 6, 1952, he treated JACOB LOWE for hemorrhoids, Oct. 19, 1963, treated LANE ANDERSON for hemorrhoids, April 14, 1966, treated SADIE MASSEY and TOM JONES for a common form of pubic lice; during the examination Sadie Massey lay on the table with her underpants pulled down to her knees. Tom Jones held her hand and smoked a cigarette. Dr. Glom said, peering through a large magnifying glass, "Vell, zee little dalinks haf made demselves right at home." He gave Sadie's pudend a little pat. Lice were contracted by Sadie Massey via EDWARD GIMMIE.

GRASSY KNOLL, in Central Park, NYC, across the walk from the statue of Robert Burns; TOM JONES and VALERIE ANDERson sat (Oct. 20, 1965) hand in hand on the knoll after spending the afternoon together walking around Greenwich Village, going to the movies at the Paris Cinema, and strolling through Central Park. The outing had been planned by LANE ANDERSON who called in sick to Brooklyn College where he taught English. He suggested that Tom Jones accompany his wife into New York for the afternoon while he (Lane) baby-sat. At the same moment Tom Jones and Valerie Anderson sat down on the grassy knoll to discuss plans for returning to Hbkn., N.J., Lane Anderson rummaged about on Tom Jones's desk in the upstairs rooms which Anderson rented to Jones. Anderson uncovered a rough draft of an erotic love poem written by Jones with the inscription "for V." Included were the lines, "The sweet, silken grotto of desire," and "fastened / Within your eyes, your body's beat and sway." As Tom Jones and Valerie Anderson walked out of the park, Lane Anderson concluded reading the poem for the seventh time and replaced it in the disorder of papers on Jones's desk. (*See PHANTOMS THAT WE CREATE*...)

GROWING HAND, an avant-garde San Francisco "little" magazine, carried (Aug. 11, 1966) by TOM JONES into the home of BLACY FALIS, at 48 Shankpntr. Rd., Ptn., Mass.; after reading a passage beginning, "Condom war ding wind juke steel wail ... Hi Thou Blind Mind!" Falis said, "Are they still writing this shit?" and threw the magazine down on the coffee table between him and Jones. Jones said, "There are two interesting pieces in it."

H

HANDS OFF TIM LEARY (slogan) button in day-glow colors, worn by unidentified young visitor to Ptn., Mass.; observed by SADIE MASSEY (July 19, 1966) at Race Pt. Bch.; in company of TOM JONES and LAURENCE FAST; Massey told them she believed the "movement" owed a debt to Leary in that he had been the first one involved with the drug (LSD-25) "who was crazy enough to want to turn everybody else on." (Massey) She explained that until the hallucinogenic drug had been introduced into Cambridge (Mass.) apts., massive cultural potential had been kept in a dormant stage by the scientific technocrats. Leary, she said, was largely responsible for making the "reawakening" possible.

HELGA'S HIDEAWAY, on Third St. in Hbkn., N.J.; bar popular with Hbkn. residents, dockworkers, and foreign seamen; also frequented by local bohemian circle, led by JACOB LOWE; proprietor of the establishment was Helga Cronkmutt, who had maintained control of the business since the middle-'thirties. During the second war, the Hideaway was one of the many centers for Nazi sympathizers in predominantly German Hbkn. Her policy, though never openly hostile to non-whites, was discriminatory. In the 1950s the Hideaway became chiefly a neighborhood bar with no political atmosphere. On the evening of Aug. 14, 1965, LARRY EARLY, Paco

Funes, JERRY DENFIELD, TOM JONES, Brian Burns, and Barbara Kearney were served another round of Heineken's beer at their table by PETER KAZANOVSKY. Larry Early interrupted his sentence to taste the new beer. Then he said, "The destruction of classical art in China is absolutely necessary if a peoples' art is ever to grow there. As Marx said, tragedy will only be possible in a classless society, and this goes for any kind of meaningful national art. The art of the dynasties was inspired by the greed and cruelty of a ruling class. The people had no contact with such courtly decorations. The art which remains from this period in Chinese history is a legacy of shame for the common man. The fact that bourgeois esthetics still finds creative nourishment in it is irrelevant." He resumed drinking his beer at the end of his speech. Paco Funes argued with his point of view on the grounds that it placed politics at the front of life's concern. Funes suggested a drug-oriented mystical approach, and referred to oriental scripture. Jerry Denfield said, "Everyone has got to do his own thing, man." Tom Jones agreed with Denfield, but Barbara Kearney and Brian Burns also had political qualifications, though they were not as implicitly radical as Early's, and concerned themselves with the Vietnam war and drug arrests.

HELLO TO YOU, title of a modern diptych, combining photography, electronics, and paint, constructed in Ptn., Mass., by RUDI TREYF. It was displayed (Aug. 1, 1966) in the home of OZZIE KLUTZ and consisted of, on the right-hand side of the double panel, a painting in realistic style of a shelf of Livre de Poche paper-covered books. The titles were clearly visible.

On the left-hand side of the panel was mounted a photograph of the same shelf of books, and the same size. However, in the photograph the titles were changed every seven seconds by means of wired lights.

HERSHEY BAR (SMALL WITH ALMONDS), part offered (Aug. 18, 1966) to TOM JONES by SADIE MASSEY when he visited her for the first time at her new address, 381 Comml. St., in Ptn., Mass.; Tom Jones was disconcerted because Sadie Massey had spent the previous night with BLACKY FALIS. While they ate the chocolate Sadie Massey said about Blacky Falis, "He makes love like a hood taking candy from a baby. He pretends that he wants to take you on his lap and instead just knocks you over. Before you know it it's through. You're much better in bed than he is." (*See RUFUS, PLEASURES OF, THE.*)

HEY LONG-HAIR! 160 I.Q. AND HIGHER? MAKE YOUR BRAIN PAY! CALL 487-0223. ASK FOR MR. RISKET, sign in shop window on Comml. St., Ptn., Mass.; seen (Aug. 21, 1966) by TOM JONES and SADIE MASSEY; Sadie Massey said, "Tom, that's disgusting. How can people be so ugly? Remember Beethoven, 'The human brain is not a salable commodity?'" Tom Jones, buffeted by the brisk current of people in the narrow street, said quickly, "What difference does it make?" He wondered what his I.Q. was and how much he could get for it.

HITLER TRIP, A, term used by TOM JONES (Sept. 10, 1966) to describe eerie occurrence involving mixed media; in conversation with LAURENCE FAST in the Foc'sle Bar, Ptn., Mass.; Jones told Fast, "I was in the Cellar (bar) listening to the Beatles on the machine, something about the shining, eternal void, when the telly flashed on without a sound. And there was Hitler and huge swastikas goose-stepping across the screen with thousands of Germans just freaking." (Jones) Fast replied, "You're a Hitler-head to begin with, ain't you?" (See OUR LOSSES NEVER SEEM HIGH ENOUGH.)

HOBOKEN PARENTS FOR PEACE, an informal organization headed by JACOB LOWE and his wife, Emily, between the years 1959–64; was an effort to promote local protest action on the part of parents having children going to school in Hbkn., N.J.

HOME RUN, humorous application of baseball term used to describe Homer (Gk. poet, circa. 700 B.C.) by LANE ANDERSON in conversation (See CZECHOSLOVAKIAN MACHINE GUNS) (July 10, 1965) in Hbkn., N.J., with TOM JONES; Anderson employed the phrase in his sentence, "I'm tired of teaching courses Home Run to Joyce. I want a modern poetry course, or the Romantics." Anderson and Jones were having a literary-academic discussion to pass the time before dinner. They also smoked two marijuana cigarettes to whet their appetites. Anderson told Jones that he felt he was going through a period in his life during which his knowledge of, and interest in, modern poetry was at its peak. He wanted badly to teach a course in the subject of modern poetry but did not desire to leave the NYC area. When he asked Jones to name for him the theorist or critic of modern poetry that he (Jones) most esteemed, Jones named William Empson. But he could not finally decide between William Empson and Richard Blackmur.

I

I HAVE A GENIUS FOR POETRY AND FILM. DOES ANYBODY WANT ME? CALL PETER, AFTER 6, 228-0636, in the personals column of *The Village Voice* (Aug. 16, 1965); placed, paid for, and written by TOM JONES at the request of his friend PETER FRITZ, who was feeling lonely and bitter about his life; ad was responded to by TUKI LEE. (*See PETER'S FUNERAL.*)

IMPARTIAL REVIEW, Am. literary review, founded in 1937; T. S. Eliot called the review "the most conspicuous" in America; gallery of contributors includes most of the best Am. & Europ. writers of the period; following is transcript of taped interview with BLACKY FALIS over WBAI-FM (NYC), conducted by EDGAR COOPER, and published (Spring, 1965):

> Cooper: You've been placed in the tradition of the American Romancers by some; others say the influence of Dos Passos, especially in your early writing, is dominant. Would you comment on these assessments?
> Falis: I think I'll leave that kind of thing to those who do it best. I will say that all I remember of Dos Passos is someone's fetus getting flushed down the toilet.
> Cooper: Well, the immediate influences are unimportant, really. But do you see yourself writing in a given tradition—from the point of view of style or method?

Falis: I can tell you this. There are a lot of hairless armpits around who'll tell you about James or Dreiser or someone else. Now, what makes my books better than theirs is that I write from my guts. I'm always probing, probing the guts and vitals, the angry, wasted nights of the psyche when you're not at all sure that the morning won't bring with it the gas pipe, the straitjacket or the stomach pump. I write because I know I'm going to die spent and oozing the black colon's pus of my culture's cancer. And I want to leave behind a record of what it was like, this slow, screaming death.

Cooper: Would it be fair, then, to say you are an apocalyptic writer?

Falis: I'm an apocalyptic person. Look, we're all terminal patients in this ward. I can tell you what's making you sick because I've got the same disease, maybe a bigger dose. At the moment some guy in Kew Gardens turns off the TV set with a shrug of disgust, I come off inside my head with the knowledge, the inescapable searing truth of what's happening inside that guy's mind: The TV patterns boring deep within him like cysts of trichinosis, seeding in the millions—one day he won't be able to turn it off, you know—and it's like a lobotomy. You see, only the hospital is your living room, or your bedroom or your office, and the doctor, some poor psychotic loon, is your wife, or your boss, your mother, or maybe a neon strobe from the bar down the street. And it takes quite a bit, you see, the knife doesn't just get in there and slice up the gray jelly, oh no: It twists and severs and lacerates for about 35 years. I bet there are fewer than a thousand people in this country over the age of 35 who aren't fatally sick. Hell, I can smell them, man. And they'll probably listen to this and say, Yeah, old Blacky's got it. He's right again. Meantime what's left of their lives is puking and gagging and straining away. I don't know whether I answered your question.

Cooper: I'm sure you have. But can *you* set them free? I mean can your writing make them realize their lost freedom?

Falis: Look, it's always Physician, Heal Thyself. If I can keep myself from dying that death. Or, dying that death, if I can use up more than my share of that death's poison, that cancer's terrible winging fury, then I can say I've made it just the smallest bit easier for you to maybe escape it.

Cooper: You've talked a lot about the cancer in the culture, today, and in your writing. Can you tell me what the writer's mission means, in terms of this? Aside from the chiefly personal solutions you've outlined?

Falis: All missions are chiefly personal. As a writer in my time I speak only for myself. I don't want to talk to you about talent. The faces are always changing. The task is always the same. See it clearly and write it as you see it. Cancer is how I see it. That's my expert diagnosis.

Cooper: Well, you must be aware that much discussion, or more precisely rumor, has been given to your personal habits of work. What is your daily writing procedure like?

Falis: This will shock a lot of people, but I keep both hands on the typewriter. And I have a kind of ritual, you know, I'm a very superstitious guy. Some days if I'm feeling bored or blocked, I smoke some pot. It's a kind of creative laxative for me.

Cooper: I know that many experts consider pot to be injurious to the imagination and its workings. Have you ever written extensively with the drug?

Falis: Look, I lived on pot for six years, during which time I did all my best writing.

Cooper: I think for many of us your best writing is still *The Palace of Pudend*, your first novel. Was *The Palace* written, or partly written, under the influence of pot?

Falis: I did the whole book when I was high. But I'm a little concerned that you have the balls to sit here and tell me I haven't written a better book since then. You know, I have 5 novels out.

Cooper: Please, I think you've misunderstood my preference. *The Palace of Pudend*, many will say, is a classic of our literature. It's a credit to your career that you've wasted no time in repeating yourself. Each of your next books has struck a new chord. But let me add that *Sons and Lovers* is my favorite Lawrence, and that was his first book.

Falis: I won't argue with your taste, Edgar. I've known you for a long time. I want you to leave this on the tape, or scrap the whole thing.

Cooper: We only have time for one last question, Blacky. Have you received any communication from the President, as was rumored you had, regarding your current best seller, *Crashed in the White House*? I refer specifically to the comic sequence involving the protagonist, Rexler, and the First Lady under the staircase in the Pentagon basement.

Falis: No, I haven't received any word from our President on that one, Edgar. But as long as you work for the CIA, you can get away with murder.

Cooper: About your current work, Blacky, what have you underway now?

Falis: All I can tell you is that it's another complete departure. The novel's set in a Tijuana cathouse, and all the dialogue comes off tapes the girls sent to me. You know, I've wanted for a long time to have a heroine on a large scale. I think this time I'm making it.

INVERTED PEPPER SHAKER, on table of Cafe Rienzi (Sept. 18, 1965) in Greenwich Village, NYC; seated at table was TUKI LEE and a girl with whom she had agreed to go to bed. Tuki Lee said, "Do you know Maggie?" "Maggie Who?" the other girl asked, inverting the pepper shaker with the sleeve of her coat as she leaned across the table; she pushed back a curl of Tuki Lee's hair which had just fallen over her face. Later that evening Lee lay in bed with PETER FRITZ. As he caressed her he noticed there were tooth marks on her right breast; he turned away with tears in his eyes, but said nothing. Tuki Lee, who was quite weary and feeling ashamed, lay her head on the back of Peter Fritz's shoulder and went to sleep. Fritz remained awake in anguish until daybreak.

J

JAR OF SPANISH OLIVES, opened (June 3, 1965) at the sink of her apt. by Ellen Early at 16 River St., Hbkn., N.J. TOM JONES was the Early's guest for dinner that evening and LARRY EARLY and Jones sat in the living room drinking Rheingold beer out of the can. A half-smoked marijuana cigarette was in the ashtray. Ellen Early brought in the jar of olives and sat down. Larry Early was explaining to Jones that he had recently shifted his chief interest from painting to photography. He mentioned increasing pressure from an incompetent administration at the high school in NYC where he taught art. Ellen Early said her husband should try harder to please his superiors, as she needed every penny to get by, and couldn't afford his being fired again. She said the two children were more expensive than her husband realized. Larry Early continued to explain his reasons, esthetic and social, for his recent interest in photography. He included in his reasons the wider accessibility of photography to the contemporary sensibility and the more expressive qualities that could be rendered on film treating the contemporary urban, industrial scene. Tom Jones ate a number of olives and was bored. The oppressive heat of the day was made unbearable by the oven burners cooking dinner. Jones could feel streams of perspiration under his shirt.

JONES, HENRY (1905–), father of TOM JONES; b. in Manhattan (NYC) to lower-middle-class Jewish family = Yonawitz; incomp. secondary-school education; grew up with aspiration to be successful merchant; failed in his own businesses 3 times; once in an attempt to distribute nationally to teenagers shoelaces that glowed in the dark, during which period (1956–57) he maintained a map of the U.S. with markers designating the cities, i.e., Houston, Detroit, in which the shoelaces had been refused; another time Jones went bankrupt (1940) in the purchase of diseased cattle and an arid drilling site in Texas. Most severe business defeat was incurred when the chain of laundromats in the East 70's–80's, NYC, was caused to go out of business by the efforts of the Chinese hand launderers in the neighborhood, directed toward pricing Jones out. After this Jones said, "I'm the first victim of the yellow menace. It's here upon us. I'll go into business with someone else's money. Let him take the risk." (1960) Jones married Miss Irene Schutz in 1939; their only child, Tom, was born in the next year. Jones admonished his son to get good marks in school, marry a rich girl, and to go into business with his uncle, Ray, a manufacturer of ladies' dresses. When his son pursued a literary career, Jones said, "I've given up on you, kid, go away. You weary me. You tire me, son. Every time I look at you I get another line in my face. I can smell pot on your breath and goyim chicks on your clothes. Just tell me one thing, you stupid punk, who's going to support you when you get old?" Until Oct. 1967 (See *RITA METER MAID.*), Jones, who is employed as a fabric wholesaler in Providence, RI., had not restored amicable relations with his son. (*See DOPPELGÄNGER.*)

JONES, TOM (1940–), Am. writer, born NYC; only child of Irene and HENRY JONES. Attended Columbia Grammar Sch. and the Riverdale Sch. for Boys. In 1957 Jones entered Columbia Univ. (B.A., 1961) and published his first poem in the student literary publication. In the same issue he contributed an essay on Wallace Stevens's "Idea of Order at Key West." In the following year Jones published poems in *Poetry Northwest, The Sewanee Review, Poetry, The Massachusetts Review,* and *Chiaroscuro*. He entered the graduate school of English at Columbia Univ. in the fall of 1961 and took lodgings at 306 Washington St., Hbkn., N.J. where he rented the top floor from LANE ANDERSON. In Hbkn., Jones became acquainted with the bohemian community loosely centered around JACOB LOWE. After the culmination of his affair with VALERIE ANDERSON, Jones moved to NYC (winter, 1966) and rented an apartment at 1265 Second Ave. By this time he was appearing regularly in several literary magazines, contributing poetry and reviews. In March of 1966 he began a relationship with SADIE MASSEY and in the spring of that year he gave up his studies at the university and went to live in Ptn., Mass., accompanied by Sadie Massey. After Sadie Massey left Ptn. to travel in Europe with BLACKY FALIS, Jones determined to stay on and begin work on a novel. (*See RITA METER MAID.*)

JOY AND HOPE ARE TRANSIENT THINGS, INDUCED BY THE INTOXICANTS OF CHANCE AND DRUGS, first sentence of entry in TOM JONES's diary (Aug. 17, 1966). Jones wrote the following after returning home from dinner at

PETER PONZINI's (See STRIPED BASS), where SADIE MASSEY told him she would spend the night with BLACKY FALIS. Complete text of entry below:

> Joy and hope are transient things, induced by the intoxicants of chance and drugs. My spirit is completely disengaged. I am leagues and years away from any goal —and even these goals seem shameful conquests. I am indifferent to my writing; I honestly do not care about it; I no longer burn to see it done. I have no money, no desire to travel. I have no friend. "Sadie, I think I must leave here soon or our chances together will be nothing."—"Perhaps, after a while, away from each other. . . ." When she filled up my life the world seemed hollow around us, as if there were no memory, no future, nothing in the present besides her. Now I feel divorced from her and everything else.
>
> There is a kind of peace in the emptiness. How fragile it is. I know that the universe is indifferent to me, that every human on earth is alone, that some few might shudder at my death. Why not suicide? It is not a matter of, "What do I have to live for?" No, it is eternal relief. I devoutly believe that my consciousness as I know it, my body certainly, would cease forever if I died this moment. Next moment. I am a coward. I think of ways to do it. This is the essence of cowardice.
>
> Once before I wanted to take my life. What caused me not to? I cannot remember. I know it was fall, I walked to the park. The air was brisk and clear. Spasms

of pain, like orgasmic waves, gripped me and let me go. I saw my body uniquely, as if from a new perspective. I was young, healthy, capable, pleasing. I remembered the praises that had spilled over me from my peers and teachers, the respect and slightly hostile recognition. My chances seemed broad then; quite suddenly, there were so many things I desired yet to accomplish. Now I am indifferent to my body's uses, my mind is stale, broken by routine, only sometimes curious.

I am not afraid of hard work and failure. I simply fail to see the point of it. I am overwrought, distracted, cast adrift.

Now I sense what is happening. Perhaps it must end here always. I wanted her to help me, save me. She couldn't. Why can't I admit it? She could not—it failed her nature to be able to—just as I failed my nature to need her so. I insist that she *would not*, chose deliberately not to. I want to believe it is her fault. It is not. Could I save myself if I vowed never to need another person in my life? To live always with expendable people... no, no, no. Nothing can help me. The wisest guru might only, should he set himself the task, bring a moment of solace. Then I would be alone in myself. Sometimes I realize that I hate myself with enormous energy. But most of the time I am only indifferent.

This tonic has achieved a small success. As I write my thoughts the doom recedes. Then suddenly the impending force seizes me, "No hope, small gifts, little desire, broken love, not even any money. No one to turn to."

And then I require to know why I cannot sit on the floor before the oven and turn on the gas. I could take four or five librium and put my head in the oven. If I had a revolver here I feel certain I would use it on myself. I could not slash my wrists, the gore prevents me. I could climb out onto the ledge and jump. Would I die? P-TOWN MAN SURVIVES TWO STORY FALL IN BASKET—yes, with my luck I'd be saved to live in a basket. I could never walk into the bay. I'm afraid.

What can I do? I can wash the dishes, wash my teeth, wash my body, make the bed. What else can I do?

I must get *this* clear in my head. It is crucial. I think that something so totally private as suicide should keep itself intact at all costs. One must not be forced into suicide: I mean: If Sadie arrives with the news that she cannot continue any longer with the way things are between us—she has found someone or something else, she has become weary or bored or hostile—then would I go back to New York City, to my aunt's apartment and jump from the terrace? Yes. Sixteen stories. Would I leave this behind me here? Mail it to Sadie? Would I care—YES YES YES I would. I know I would jump. Mail this in a letter, then jump from my aunt's sixteenth-story terrace. I would get drunk or high and do it.

But will I do it anyway? If she does not bring things to a fine point, will I? Will I tell her I am going and do it anyway? Will I kill myself then? Or if she seems glad to see me? How can I be sure? I must not let my own life be a function of another's disposition. I must either decide to do it in any case, or not. And if not, I must try to find some reason or way for my life. THIS must not be allowed to continue, as it can, for years or a lifetime. Those in wards live like this. I shall die of cancer of the brain.

Either I must take action and kill myself or find a way to live.

Below, in a worse hand, Jones scrawled the following lines:

> In a dry corner peace whispers
> And shrinks away.
> Death's head sings sweetly to me
> Images of free-fall, my body
> White and topsy-turvy in the sun
> Flung from a terrace on the sixteenth
> Floor in freedom.
> O, preserve the moment, my indifference
> Clamours to be shattered.

K

KAZANOVSKY, PETER (PETEY) (1904–), Russo-Am. bartender; emigrated to U.S. in 1925; found employment as dockhand in Hbkn., N.J., where he later settled. Tended bar in several Hbkn. establishments frequented by the local bohemian circle, including The Triangle Bar, HELGA'S HIDEAWAY, and #11 River St. He married Miss Irene Schlimmer in 1932.

KEEP ME HIGH AND I'LL BALL YOU FOREVER, a (slogan) button in psychedelic patterns designed (July 4, 1966) by SADIE MASSEY and sold (July 29, 1966) to Eddie Jaickel (*See MOLE*) for duplication and distribution at Friendly's Esso Station, Ptn., Mass.

KILLER, type of individual TOM JONES suggested PETER FRITZ was not; in conversation (July 8, 1965) at a table in The Kettle of Fish Bar, NYC where they drank Budweiser beer; Fritz described his chagrin at being refused for military service by the US Army the previous afternoon. Fritz told how he was willing to enlist for combat duty in Vietnam. Jones said he was "deeply shocked" and questioned whether Fritz was being honest with him. Fritz complained that he was upset over the moral and intellectual laxity overcoming his generation, particularly evidenced by the behavior of individuals in Greenwich Village (N.Y.C.). He said he doubted whether America could survive in a hostile world without "an inner-core of responsibility." (Fritz) Jones expressed amazement at his friend's new convictions. "You make it seem as if I never knew you. When did this all start happening to your head, Peter?" (Jones) He asked Fritz, "Do you really want to go to Asia and kill people? You're no killer." Fritz insisted that his words reflected a maturity in his thinking. He agreed that perhaps he and Jones had never understood each other. Fritz said, "Maybe you're one of them, too. Look at them! (Fritz gestured through the window to the crowd on MacDougal St.) They're supposed to be free? Artists? They all dress alike. They all sound alike. What do they know about poetry, anyway? Do you think they know what Landor wrote? or Christopher Smart? Do you think they care?" After this outburst he broke down and guietly sobbed, resting his head on the table. When he recovered he said, "I am willing to die for my country if our leaders say they need my life. You should be ashamed of yourself if you feel differently. In other countries people like you are kept in prisons, without even the chance to work. Here you can do what you like." Jones told Fritz he couldn't understand whether he was being "put on," but that if he (Fritz) was being serious, Jones was at a loss to begin to offer advice. Fritz said, "OK, Tom. I'll call you in a few days when I'm feeling better." Fritz left the bar and Jones remained holding his head in his hands.

KLUTZ, OSWALD (OZZIE) (1907-), Am. millionaire and patron of the arts; speculations on commodities exchange cornered world soya bean market during World War II. Educated in NYC public schools and School of Dentistry, N.Y.U.

Retired from dental practice after making fortune and traveled widely in Europe and the Far East. Private collection of 20th-cent. painting noted for its inclusiveness but inferior quality. Honorary degrees from N.Y.U., Yale Univ., and Princeton Univ. Sponsor of Miss Catherine Petú (who became his wife in 1951), Hyman Hyman, and RUDI TREYF. Since 1960, Klutz has divided his time between NYC and Ptn., Mass., where his home is a gathering place for contemporary artists.

KNITTED BERET (BLUE), kneaded in the hands of LAURENCE FAST (Aug. 11, 1966) in Ptn., Mass.; Fast was in conversation with BLACKY FALIS and TOM JONES, explaining his attitude toward his prison experiences. Fast said, "When I was in prison, man, I got to understand how to use my time. That's the whole secret. If you know how to use your time, you can keep on being a person. 'Cause otherwise the Place and the System are gonna get down on you and break you. The cats I went in with all got out before me. They were bored, man, bored crazy and they just didn't know what to do with their time. They started to feel like cons, and man, when that happened they got switched off forever. 'Cause a con is Inferior, and nobody's gonna let you forget it. Sure, they served a few months less time than I did but, man, those guys went back inside, all of them, within six months. I didn't get no time off for good conduct or nothin'. I served all my time and those people in there respected me, 'cause I never stopped being a man. The whole secret is to keep your self-respect by filling up your time." (Fast)

L

LATER, contemporary expression remarked on (July 19, 1966) by BLACKY FALIS in the question, ". . . why do you say 'later' to some people and 'goodbye' to others?" addressed to TOM JONES. The two were walking on Comml. St., Ptn., Mass., after leaving the home of OSWALD KLUTZ. Jones replied that the slang term cheated bourgeois expectations of social regularity which requires a fixed time and place. He gave as an example the sentence, "I'll meet you *there* on Wednesday at 6 p.m." Jones went on to say, "*Later* implies that such trivia as time and place of the next meeting will take care of themselves, and this is usually true."

LAW OF DIMINISHING RETURNS, frequently cited by TOM JONES as a governing force in his relationships with women; first usage, fall 1965, as applied to his abortive love affair with VALERIE ANDERSON. Jones at this time had been a resident for 4 years at the Anderson home. Phrase also used by Jones to describe his relationship with SADIE MASSEY. (*See STRIPED BASS.*)

LEATHER ADDRESS BOOK (RED CORDOVAN), belonging to SADIE MASSEY, used by her (Aug. 29, 1966) to write poem in, Race Pnt., Ptn., Mass.; Massey had found herself in a contemplative mood and walked to Race Pnt. Her despair for the end of the world, encouraged by her relationships with

BLACKY FALIS and TOM JONES, was nevertheless mitigated by a feeling of an all-pervading love. Text of poem, written in pencil in address book, follows: (untitled)

> Explosions shake the firedomed towns, untowered
> fiercely burning in the nova light, cobalt blue,
> after the last screams, many hours after that,
> seething in a jet of particles, lightyears high,
>   irradiated
> are the voices of Babel, from every atomized
>   earth-man's land,
> voices of a lotus-like tenderness and deep
>   compassion,
> pulsing in the common measure, the eternal fire
>   and ice;
> These voices are the joy and grief that no one bears,
> the immense fraternity among the hideous dying,
>   not somber
> but serene, a smile of witness without remorse,
>   testifying
> softly until
> finally words were no longer necessary.

LEE, TUKI (1940–), Oriental-Am. bohemian; born and raised in NYC of Japanese parentage; formal education ended with high school; left home at age 16. Well-known among Greenwich Village coffee-house habituées, and frequenter of other haunts of disaffected youth. Answered ad in personals column of *The Village Voice* (Aug. 16, 1965) (*See* I HAVE A GENIUS . . .) placed by TOM JONES for his friend PETER FRITZ.

She and Fritz formed an alliance lasting to his death (Oct. 2, 1965) (*See PETER'S FUNERAL*). Tuki Lee's irregular behavior, including frequent lesbian activity (*See INVERTED PEPPER SHAKER*) and use of addictive narcotics, i.e., amphetamine and heroin, along with Peter Fritz's passionate attachment to her, caused him severe remorse which resulted in his taking his life. Tuki Lee left N.Y. to live in San Francisco.

LESSON OF THE MASTER, THE (1892), short story by Henry James, alluded to by TOM JONES in conversation with BLACKY FALIS (Sept. 7, 1966) at a table in the Old Colony Bar, Ptn., Mass.; Falis told Jones, "You've got a good head, Kid. Why don't you use it? You're not going to get anywhere scratching out poems. Do a novel. Put into it all your ideas. Write a new kind of book. (*See NEW YORK TIMES BOOK REVIEW.*) You've got what it takes. My mind's so slow I can catch it trying to climb out of the rut it's in. What wisdom is there in being able to manipulate the masturbatory fantasies of invented people? I'm stale but in my guts I have to keep writing, it's like a disease. I'm taking Sadie away from you because she's my only chance, the only one who can make me believe in myself again. I've raised the ante, now I'll see what I've been holding all these years." (Falis) After a pause Jones alluded, "So this is The Lesson of the Master. You even get to keep the girl. I would rather be a businessman than write novels." (Jones) (*See RITA METER MAID.*)

LIST OF BOOKS, on TOM JONES's bookshelf (606 Comml. St.) Ptn., Mass.; (June-Oct., 1966); from top to bottom, left to right: *On Aggression, One Flew Over the Cuckoo's Nest, The Inhab-*

ited Universe, Necessary Doubt, Nightwood, Reich: Selected Writings, The Recognitions, Chief Mod. Poets of Eng. and Am., A Clockwork Orange, Shadow of Fu Manchu, Exploring the Occult, Hindemith: A Composer's World, The Upanishads, Whitehead: Modes of Thought, Speak, Memory, Perspectives #2, Magic Books from Mexico, Magister Ludi, Laughter in the Dark, Groucho and Me, New Directions #17, 4 Existentialist Theologians, Soc. Hist. of Art (4 vols.), *7 Yrs. in Tibet, Gestalt Therapy, Collected Later Poems of W. C. Williams, Buccdancer's Choice, Lao Tzu, The Empire City, Shakespeare's Works* (4 vols.), *The Divided Self, The Erasers, Dawn of Magic, Meet My Maker The Mad Molecule, Biology of Mind.*

LOOP OF HAIR, habitually twisted around index finger by LANE ANDERSON; this gave the appearance of tiny curls along the back of his neck. Anderson twisted his hair (April 19, 1965) and spoke to TOM JONES, who sat with him in the Circle Bar, Hbkn., N.J.; the jukebox continued to play the same Beatles recording. PETER KAZANOVSKY delivered another round of beers to the table as Anderson told Jones, "Music just isn't the same any more. There are no melodies, just blah blah blah. Some of the things are even savage." Jones said, "It's true that much of this music is densely recorded, but this creates its own effect." He went on to foresee brilliant developments in electronic rock music. Anderson objected on the grounds that no rock music could ever excel "musically" even the dance music of the 1940s. He claimed that the rock musicians had no control over their instruments and that they only made noise. Jones said, "It's useless to argue with you."

He said that the ground of music had changed, had become electronic, and that the music "would await it's audience." In answer to the query by Anderson as to whether he thought that rock music would ever become as compositionally difficult as chamber music, Jones said, "I don't think how hard it is to write a certain piece of music has any connection with how good it is."

LOST WORLDS, the possibility of the existence of which was discussed (June 1, 1966) by TOM JONES and SADIE MASSEY, in the BEACON HOTEL, NYC; topic inspired by viewing of late-night movie on TV, *Ice-Men of Atlantis*; Jones suggested that the lost world, Scheria, mentioned by Homer in the *Odyssey* and that cited by Plato in the *Crito* evoked Tartessos (Old Tes. = Tarshish) at the mouth of the Guadalquivir R., Spain. Jones explained that, after flourishing for a number of centuries as a depository of wealth and wisdom, the culture vanished without a trace, c. 500 B.C.

LOWE, JACOB (1913–), Am. novelist, poet, psychologist, composer, film critic, and political scientist; b. & grew up in NYC; in Bronx middle-class Jewish household, father was house painter; mother was piano teacher; B.A. N.Y.U. (1933) & Ph.D. Univ. of Chicago (1934); married Emily Kleiner, 1938; dghtr. b. 1950; Lowe's prolific output and varied talents soon brought him to the attention of literary and academic community, but his outspoken opinions on politics and sex limited his audience to the avant-garde. It was not until early 1960s that Lowe became unofficial spokesman for rebellious Am. youth. He achieved an almost overnight success and most of his books were given new editions. Aside from his writing Lowe became a popular lecturer, bringing his controversial views to a large segment of Am. college youth; he has appeared often on network TV and radio, frequently to the embarrassment of the media. Lowe has been active in popularizing the form of public protest, esp. in regard to the spread of nuclear weapons and the war in Vietnam. His best known works include *The Sons of Freedom* (1943), a long philosophical novel setting forth the idea of a practical utopia in which sexual polymorphism, intellect, and commerce would flourish side by side, derived from the Athenian and Platonic ideals; *How It Is* (1959), a collection of important essays showing the extent to which obsolete cultural-political institutions have corrupted their original purpose; and *Reality Masters* (1964), a personal anthology of prose, poetry, anecdotes, and psychological observations. Lowe entered group psychotherapy with a small group of his own, including such members as LANE ANDERSON, JERRY DENFIELD, and LARRY EARLY. His influence over his analysands extended to community proportions and for several years Lowe acted as central force behind bohemian colony located in Hbkn., N.J. *Esquire Mag.* (July, 1963) said, "Through the corridors of importance and the antechambers of the avant-garde, the name of Jacob Lowe resounds as a byword for political and sexual freedom."

LOW TIDE, title of a poem written by TOM JONES (Aug. 25, 1966). Jones walked along the beach from 381 Comml. St., Ptn., Mass., where he had been visiting SADIE MASSEY, to his residence at 606 Comml. St.; he composed the poem in his head as he went along. In mid-August, Sadie Massey had left their place of joint residence at 606 Comml. St. and taken her own apt. Jones was disturbed by this and other aspects of her behavior in this period. The full text of the poem follows:

> *low tide*
>   for S.
>
> the bay has an empty grin
> the moon's yellow stain
> bleeds on the water like refuse
>
> a rusting breakwater groans in the wind
> escaping birds shriek over the cold sand
>
> the black wharf pilings are like cigars
> stubbed out
> and the stars breathe like mirrors
> showing deserts of within
>
> a red-eyed crippled dog comes near
> if I put out my hand will he bite?

LSD (lysergic acid diethylamide), the properties and characteristics of which were summed up (Aug. 10, 1966) by TOM JONES and SADIE MASSEY, in conversation with PETER PONZINI, in Ptn., Mass.; Jones explained that the chemical was brought to the tissues by the blood, and consequently went to all parts and layers of the brain. It thus caused disturbances in normal sensory perception by exciting the functioning neurons to faster thought processes, with definite leaps, in which the quantitative moment had the decisive role. Jones observed this was evident in the social behavior of those who had taken the drug; he said the similarities in the behavior of clinically designated schizophrenics might be due to the "leap" in the electric impulses generated by LSD. Massey explained that excitations in the layer of the cortex where visual experiences were engrammed led to hallucinations, caused by random, autonomous deviations in which elements were correlated with previous contents of consciousness. Ponzini inquired, in the light of his long history in state mental institutions, whether it would be advisable for him to experiment with the drug. Massey and Jones found this a difficult question, but agreed it would be advisable in a controlled environment. They disagreed as to the type of environment best for Ponzini.

LSD NOT LBJ, automobile bumper sticker, seen (Aug. 7, 1966) by TOM JONES and SADIE MASSEY, in Ptn., Mass.; "Yeah," exclaimed Massey, "that's just how I feel!" Jones agreed heartily, "Me too." Both of them believed that Johnson was involved in the murder of Kennedy and they felt that the reawakening powers of LSD would be beneficial to society at large.

M

MASSEY, SADIE (1947–), b. Rye, NY; precocious childhood as only daughter of prominent international banker and Long Island socialite marked by bitter differences of opinion on her upbringing; Massey refused conventional systems of education and insisted on private tutors, each skilled in an area of her interests. Thus became accomplished in languages, science, literature, and the arts. In 1965, when only 18, purchased penthouse at BEACON HOTEL, NYC, where she set up independent household and devoted herself to further self-realization. After making acquaintance of TOM JONES in NYC, she traveled with him to Ptn., Mass. (summer, 1966). In fall of that year, she left for Europe with BLACKY FALIS, where she remained until her world-famous journey to Tibet (1967).

MEDITATION ON LIFE AND DEATH, serious and sustained reflection, engaged in (June 4, 1966) by BLACKY FALIS in Ptn., Mass.; Falis contemplated origin of the universe in whirling hydrogen wastes, colliding whorls in the cosmic void. He recalled an undergraduate attempt at an ode to the carbon atom, Creator of Life. He was aware of certain ironies, i.e., that breathing vegetables were responsible for the ozone layer. But he was unable to resist the pull toward seeing all life and non-life as fundamentally the same. He grasped that life was inherent in all matter, from the primordial hydrogen atom to bacteria which do not need oxygen, to man. He was equally assured that he would never reconcile himself to a view of man's life as having any purpose whatever in a cosmic design. Too great was the opposite conviction that the entire universe was the result of the blind groping of chemical reactions. However, he accepted his own death in terms of his perception of the cosmological immensity in which his own existence participated. Falis was unable, despite his philosophical convictions, to abandon the habit of carrying secretly on his person at all times a pocket syringe containing a lethal dosage of morphine to avoid the physical pain of a violent accident.

MINOS, KING OF THE BRONZE AGE, title of film seen (June 29, 1966) by TOM JONES and SADIE MASSEY in Orleans, Mass.; Jones had borrowed PETER PONZINI's Ford to drive up Cape to Orleans; Jones and Massey smoked marijuana as they drove in the car. Later they ate clam rolls and drank beer purchased at a roadside stand. As they were leaving the movie theater Sadie Massey asked why the Bronze Age had preceded the Iron Age since iron is more common and easier to make than bronze, which is an alloy of copper and tin. Tom Jones said he had no idea. But he added that it was his opinion that scientists were not able to agree on even approximate dates for the Bronze Age.

MOISTENING PUDEND, experienced by ALICE FAITH (July 21, 1966) during the nightclub performance of her lover, LAURENCE FAST, at the Crown and Anchor, Ptn., Mass.; Faith sat at a table with TOM JONES and SADIE MASSEY; Faith told Massey of her growing sexual excitement. Massey replied, "I think that's very sweet." She proceeded to expertly bring Faith to orgasm by touching her under the table. Following is partial transcript of Fast's nightclub act:

Look, baby, this country was founded on race hatred. That's where the poison is, in your roots! 4 million red men exterminated. Genocide. It's still going down, baby. ⅓ of the casualties in Vietnam and ¼ of the combat troops is black. Did you know that? So like this time it's black men exterminating yellow men—in the interests of those same red-neck crackers who balled my grandmother. Dig it? . . .

There's been a lot of talk lately about guerrillas trained by our Native Sons in Vietnam who come back to the ghettos with both their arms and legs. And I know a lot of cats are stashing shit all over the place, machine guns from Czechoslovakia, hand grenades, duffle bags full of grass for currency to arm the Brothers. Is there going to be a war? Dig it: the Brothers are learning to organize, snipe, burn down people's homes with Ronson lighters, just like over in Vietnam. If white America doesn't suddenly wake up by the '68 elections—and our boys are going to be comin' home by then—the whole generation is going to be one long, violent, hot summer winter fall and spring . . . Did you ever dig this, man? A couple of miles from Watts the streets are crawling with Flower Children. Flower-power, baby, they say.

Flower-power. Now I'm not puttin' down the hippies, I know they've said Fuck off to President Johnson, too. And I know the cops get down on them sometimes and stomp them. But, baby, if it gets too severe, you can always cop your daddy's check at the P.O. and take that first bus home. You can go back to being white, dig it? But a lot of Brothers can't split Watts so easily. And that's why we need Black Power . . .

The Brothers are waking up to this shit, Whitey, and you better, too. Don't come selling us no birth control, we want to GROW, baby. We don't dig you tellin' us, Well, just cool it with these pills, Mr. Brown. Uh-uh. You dig it? The white folks are very up-tight with the thought of 10 million more little black bastards rooting around in their daughter's panties. No, sir, Mr. Brown. We're livin' in the Great Society, baby, and since no one asked us what that should mean, I think we ought to just groove and find out . . .

MOLE, brown, discovered (Aug. 9, 1966) on upper left thigh of Sister Louise Toggata, the "Singing Nun," during "gang bang" on Race Pnt. Bch., Ptn., Mass.; mole was first noticed by Eddie Jaickle, a gas-station attendant, and the sixth person to mount Sister Louise during the night's encounter. Eddie Jaickle said, "Hey, look man, the nun has a mole." Arthur Morris, proprietor of the Kiddy Wear Store, Ptn., Mass., said humorously, "Shit, no, that's where I put out my cigarette." Sister Toggata had been appearing nightly in Ptn. as an entertainer after receiving national prominence as a popular singer in the spring of 1966. Sister Toggata resigned from the Order of Sisters of the Immaculate Sacred Bleeding Heart later in the month of August and traveled to Hollywood to make a picture about her life. Sister Superior Elizabeth Regge, recalling the time spent by Sister Toggata in the order, said, "the entire convent (Framingham, Ill.) will miss her," and "will anxiously await the release of the movie based on Sister Toggata's life with us as a bride of Christ." Sister Toggata recorded her biggest success (1,000,000 sales) in April, 1966, with her version of "Lord, What a Morning!"

MONOPOLY GAME, a popular Am. board game, the object of which is to force the other players into bankruptcy; one such game was played (July 21, 1966) in the afternoon in Ptn., Mass.; TOM JONES and SADIE MASSEY, ALICE FAITH, LAURENCE FAST, and ZEKE SAWYER were the participants. The game lasted three hours and fifty-eight minutes with Sawyer emerging as the winner on a roll of the dice which carried Alice Faith's token (a tiny metal cannon) onto Boardwalk where Sawyer had hotels. Though technically able to raise the funds to pay her debt, to do so would have destroyed her holdings, and she found it wiser to resign immediately. She was encouraged in her decision by the rest of the players, especially Laurence Fast who had a nightclub engagement to play at eight o'clock that night. The game had begun with several players contesting the ownership of the better monopolies while Faith and Sawyer concentrated on gaining controlling interests of the less valuable properties. This they accomplished, beginning with a trade which sent Connecticut Ave. to Sawyer in return for St. Charles Place. Building on their respective properties continued until Faith and Sawyer each had constructed hotels which threatened to put the other players out of the game early. Through the efforts of Tom Jones, neither of the leading players was able to deliver the coup de grace until Sadie Massey, who had become bored, made a gift of some cash to Sawyer giving him sufficient funds to put hotels on his properties.

MUSTACHE COMMERCIAL, THE, title of film by Lynn Ratener, viewed by LANE ANDERSON and TOM JONES (Aug. 26, 1965) (*See LES DYSTROPHES*); screened as a short, the film depicted a young man who shaves off his mustache with a Gillette Techmatic razor and Noxema shaving cream, while smoking Lark cigarettes and drinking a Budweiser beer. Anderson and Jones were amused by the film. The contrast in tone with *Les Dystrophes* disturbed Anderson.

N

NAVY WORK SHIRT, purchased (April 14, 1965) by LANE ANDERSON at the Hbkn. Surplus Store, Wash. St., Hbkn., N.J.; in the company of TOM JONES, who purchased shoelaces. Anderson examined a Navy pea coat which revealed a cluster of 3 bullet holes in the upper back. He attempted to engage the proprietor, Morris Greenberg, in a dialogue concerning the Am. War in Vietnam, but Greenberg refused to give an opinion. Anderson told Jones as they were leaving the surplus store that JACOB LOWE had been invited to address a group of govt. internal policy planners that evening in Wash., D.C. Anderson said, "This is really what you call 'managing dissent,' but Jacob always appears at these things. At least it's covered the next morning in the Wash. papers. And he always blasts them, calls them greedy butchers, the whole thing." (Anderson) As they approached 307 Wash. St., Jones reminded Anderson that he had left behind his newly purchased Navy work shirt in the surplus store. Together they walked back to retrieve it.

NEW YORK TIMES SUNDAY BOOK REVIEW, wadded into ball and thrown (Aug. 23, 1966) into the fireplace by BLACKY FALIS in his home on Shankpntr. Rd., Ptn., Mass.; Falis said to TOM JONES, who was visiting with SADIE MASSEY, that he wondered often why novels had continued to be written;

NINE

he pointed to the deadness on the contemporary scene. Tom Jones remarked that he would like to write a novel combining travel-writing with alternating passages of hard-core pornography. He said he imagined the characters traveling in the East, perhaps to the sacred temples of Khajooraho, Bundelkhand, where there are well-known erotic representations. As an example of the kind of travel-writing he had in mind he mentioned the books of Fosco Mariani. Later the same afternoon, while Falis and Massey surreptitiously held hands in one corner of Falis's study, Jones examined a paper-covered book he had drawn from the shelves. He quoted from it aloud to Falis (Compass C31, *The Craft of Fiction*, by Percy Kubbock): "As quickly as we read a book, it melts and shifts in the memory; even at the moment when the page is turned, a great part of the book, its finer detail, is already vague and doubtful. A little later, after a few days or months, how much is really left of it? A cluster of impressions, some clear points emerging . . . is all we can hope to possess." Jones asked Falis why someone hadn't written a novel made up entirely of these "clusters of impressions," since they were all that remained, regardless of the manner of composition. (*See* LESSON OF THE MASTER, THE.)

NINE, number, the significance of which was alluded to by SADIE MASSEY in conversation with BLACKY FALIS (Aug. 5, 1966) at the Atlantic House, in Ptn., Mass.; in presence of ALICE FAITH, LAURENCE FAST, TOM JONES and PETER PONZINI. Group was seated at rear table drinking beers. Falis objected to Massey's "glib run-around with numerology" (Falis) and commented that she tried too hard to make a mystery of herself. Massey said angrily, "You don't know anything about me or numerology. In Revelations, the number of the beast . . . is the number of a man. That's 666. Which adds up to 18, which is 9. The Sidereal Year is 25,920 years. This adds up to 9 and is the sum of the equinoctial precession, the ratio of which is 72, and adds up to 9. All the minutes of a day and all the seconds add up to 9. There are 1,440 minutes (here Falis interjected, "Stop," but Massey continued) and 86,400 seconds. Any number of degrees of equinotical precession adds up to 9: 2 degrees is 144 years, 10 degrees is 720 years. The mean normal respiration rate is 18 times a minute, the pulse is 72. The average number of heart beats in an hour is 4,320 and respirations in an hour is 1,080. They all add to 18 or 9. In a day your heart beats an average 103,690 times and that's 9, too. In a day your respirations average 25,920, the number of the Sidereal Year. Is all this coincidence? Let him who hath understanding, and all that. The number of the beast is the number of a man. (Rev. XIII: 18)" (Massey)

O

ONE ARGUMENT AGAINST ART, requested by BLACKY FALIS of SADIE MASSEY (Aug. 4, 1966) in his parked car on Shankpntr Rd., Ptn., Mass.; Massey replied, "To be a great composer means to anticipate with genius the possible combinations of sounds. But what about that person who hears only one sound perfectly and can reproduce it? My argument is, if he heard one sound perfectly, he would have no need to reproduce it." Falis told Massey that such an attitude was inconsistent with "all the other ego games you play." (Falis)

OPIO (Sp. = opium), labeled pharmaceutical jar made of ceramic material and painted blue; opened (June 11, 1966) by SADIE MASSEY who used it to keep marijuana near her bedside, at the BEACON HOTEL, NYC; Massey filled a long wooden pipe with marijuana from the opio jar and handed it to TOM JONES. She told Jones, "In Mexico this jar and the grass in it would cost you a dollar and a quarter." Jones said, "I've been to Mexico."

ORANGE MANILA FOLDER, carried by Samuel Blackstone (July 21, 1966) to the house of OSWALD KLUTZ in Ptn., Mass.; the envelope contained photographs that Blackstone had printed of SADIE MASSEY wearing body paint. (It is not known who took the photographs.) When Blackstone entered the Klutz living room RUDI TREYF and Hyman Hyman, who were talking together, asked Blackstone did he have the photographs. Blackstone said he had given the envelope to Klutz. After Klutz had examined the color photographs he carried them in the folder to the enclosed porch where the Falises were talking to TOM JONES and Sadie Massey. MARJORIE FALIS asked Massey, "who took these?" Jones said, "No one knows." Massey added, "I used to wear body paint at parties." BLACKY FALIS said, "I'd love to clean the brushes." (*See ELEVEN WEST HUDSON ST.*)

ORGIES, topic of brief conversation betw. LANE and VALERIE ANDERSON, in their bedroom (Sept. 10, 1965), Hbkn., N.J.; L. Anderson told his wife, "Sometimes I'd like it if you'd be more cruel when we made love." When his wife replied she did not enjoy being cruel, L. Anderson said, "We should start going to more orgies, Valerie." He entered into a reverie of his youth and the orgies he had enjoyed with the Being Theatre group. V. Anderson asked her husband whether JACOB LOWE ever participated in the orgies. L. Anderson said, "He always fled. There was something disturbing in it for him." He explained his belief in terms of "Jacob's serene tolerance of all kinds of sex," (L. Anderson) and stated, "Jacob has what mathematicians call an elegant mind. It transcends any part of himself that may be lacking." V. Anderson left the room to attend to the child.

OUR LOSSES NEVER SEEM HIGH ENOUGH, isolated sentence, attributed to Adolf Hitler; read (July 15, 1966) by TOM JONES, aloud to SADIE MASSEY, in the Foc'sle Bar, Ptn., Mass.; this and another sentence attributed to Goering, "When I hear anyone speaking of culture I draw my revolver," were read by Jones from the book *The Dawn of Magic*, by Louis Pauwels and Jacques Bergier, 1963, Gibbs and Phillips, Ltd.; Jones read these sentences aloud because he was astounded by them. He told Massey that the book contained much information concerning the cosmological world-theories which informed Nazi thinking. Said Jones, "These guys were so spaced out that it's unbelievable they were running a country. Their thing was to serve the Powers of Evil and destroy civilization, and then start *another* civilization of superior men." Massey said, overcome with mirth, "The Brain Police, The Brain Police."

OVEN KNIFE, used by TOM JONES (Sept. 5, 1966) to separate a twin-pack of Nabisco Mallomar Cookies; in his residence Ptn., Mass.; upon tasting the first Mallomar Jones experienced *déjà vu*; he recalled VALERIE ANDERSON and another Mallomar twin-pack. Later he said, "Who is Valerie? What is she? Is she deeply sensitive, fragile, and pure, a Botticelli madonna with child, that her husband thinks she is? a blonde with round heels? a petty bitch?" (*See* GRASSY KNOLL, LAW OF DIMINISHING RETURNS, PURPLE DRESS, THREE BOILED POTATOES, WEDDING BAND, WOOL SWEATER, *and* DOOM.)

P

PANAMA RED, a variety of *Cannabis sativa* grown in Panama and so designated by its rusty hue; several cigarettes of which were smoked (Aug. 13, 1966) by ZEKE SAWYER and TOM JONES in Sawyer's apt. in the Inn of the Dunes Motel, Ptn., Mass.; Sawyer told Jones that on three occasions he and a friend of his who owned a private plane had flown two hundred kilos of marijuana from a plantation near Panama City to Akron, Ohio. Jones listened appreciatively and then promised to tell Sawyer a story which would "Blow his mind" (Jones). The story he told concerned the owner of a small fishing boat in the Florida Keys in the months before the Cuban Revolution (1958). Approached by revolutionaries who offered to pay him to transport munitions to Cuba, he soon became involved with the shipment of men and arms in large quantities. He was making as many as five round trips each week between Cuba and Key West, Florida. By this time the revolutionaries had gone into debt beyond their capacity to pay and offered him double what they owed payable when the revolution had been accomplished. The fishing boat captain assumed the risk to see it through. When the revolution succeeded, the men with whom he had been associated told him that they were unable to give him cash but would give him $80,000 (U.S.) in cocaine. They also promised to establish a residence and place of business for him in Los Angeles, Calif., which they did. Along with the sizable amount of cocaine, there was on the premises a small arsenal comprising grenades, bazookas, Czechoslovakian-made submachine guns, ammunition, and dynamite (TNT). The fishing boat captain had nearly sold his quantity of cocaine and was preparing to fly to Greece, when an acquaintance asked him for some marijuana for a friend of his who had never smoked any. This last person, a college freshman, was discovered with the drug by his father, who called the police. Under police pressure the fishing boat captain's friend was located and made to disclose the identity of the person who had originally sold the $5 (U.S.) package of marijuana. When the police raided his place, expecting to find some marijuana, they came upon the entire storehouse of drugs and armaments. The fishing boat captain was sentenced to thirty years. Zeke Sawyer admitted that the story was a "mind-bender." (Sawyer)

PAPAGENO, 6-months-old kitten (*Felis domesticus*) named for char. in Mozart's opera, *Die Zauberflöte;* mother was TIFFANY; killed accidentally, by LANE ANDERSON (June 9, 1966), by mutilation, in workings of Castro-convertible sofa, in SADIE MASSEY's apt. in BEACON HOTEL, NYC (*See DOOM*); sofa was opened by Anderson and TOM JONES immed. prior to having intercourse with Massey (alternately and at the same time), the night previous (8th). (*See BISHOP'S COPE.*) When Jones and Massey retired to bedroom, Anderson remained on living-room sofa. Following aft. (9th) Papageno was trapped in metal bars when Anderson attempted to fold sofa closed. Death was not immed. discovered; after a search began when the kitten did not appear at dinner, Jones spotted protruding cat's tail at rear of sofa; Jones and Beacon Hotel janitor removed the body and incinerated it.

PENNY, referred to (Aug. 17, 1966) by SADIE MASSEY at home of PETER PONZINI in Ptn., Mass.; used in anecdote illustrating man's evolution; in conversation with BLACKY FALIS, TOM JONES and Peter Ponzini. Falis and Jones were discussing political developments when Massey interrupted with her anecdote. She said to imagine a penny placed on top of a postage stamp, both on top of Cleopatra's Needle. She explained that the age of the earth was represented by the 70-ft. column, the entire period of man's existence by the coin, and the length in which he has been slightly civilized by the stamp; a column of stamps a mile high would indicate the period during which life is possible on earth. Massey said, "What do you care how things are juggled now or in a thousand years? If man survives he will only fulfill himself in several hundreds of thousands of years. Anything coming before that is semiprimitivism. Now what do you care about the future of your movement or a ruling elite? Just cool it and do your own thing." She said that man was on the verge of an entire restructuring of ideas on his role in the universe. Drugs and cybernetics, she said, were opening new vistas of potential; she added, "... if men can once learn that there are shortcuts to the final evolution—this is what cybernetics is about—a general level of experience will be attained higher than what all but a few must possess today." (Massey) (*See* STRIPED BASS.)

PERCEPTION OF THE INFINITE, maintained by TOM JONES (July 23, 1966) in a discussion with BLACKY FALIS, SADIE MASSEY, and LAURENCE FAST to be the origin of religious feeling, in Ptn., Mass.; Sadie Massey said the origin of religious feeling was in death, and Falis said it was "probably some kind of animism." Fast kept silent on the issue until pressed by Jones and Falis, when he said, "I believe what's written in the Koran." Jones went on to qualify his statement by adding that his definition of "perception" was a very general one.

PETER'S FUNERAL (PETER FRITZ), held on Oct. 4, 1965, at Riverside Mem. Chapel, NYC; TOM JONES arrived a few minutes before ten o'clock and took a seat in one of the back pews; he recognized several students from Columbia Univ. who had been classmates of his and Fritz's. A woman dressed in black in the first pew wept continually and would not be comforted. Jones did not expect to see TUKI LEE nor did he. She had called him on Oct. 2, saying that Fritz had been found in Tompkins Sq. Pk., a few blocks from where he lived, with his throat slashed from ear to ear. No one knew how long he had been dead. She concurred with the police that the death had been a suicide. Lee said she was leaving town, and hung up. A rabbi, who confessed he hadn't known Fritz well, read a brief service from II Isaiah. The coffin containing Fritz's body was closed.

PHANTOMS THAT WE CREATE FOR OURSELVES, topic of conversation (Sept. 28, 1965) held betw. LANE ANDERSON and JACOB LOWE in the San Remo Bar (NYC); Anderson told Lowe that he was still haunted by feelings of inadequacy and was often unable to achieve an erection during the sex act. He said he knew these were figures created by his guilt at being secretly unworthy. Jacob Lowe replied that he, too, often was unable to have an erection, but suggested that Anderson's difficulties could be explained in another way. Lowe said, "Certainly, Lane (Anderson), though moral-masochism is a term we don't like to employ, . . . you do torment yourself continually. But are you sure that all of your phantoms are schiz-y? Are you certain that boy, Jones, is only platonic with Valerie?" (*See GRASSY KNOLL.*)

PICTURE TUBE (TV), shattered on carpet of FALIS living room in Ptn., Mass.; TV was overturned (Aug. 20, 1966) by MARJORIE FALIS upon learning that her husband was carrying on an affair with SADIE MASSEY; this information was revealed directly to Marjorie Falis by her husband, during a quarrel. Observing his wife fall into a rage and smash the TV, BLACKY FALIS left the house without avoidable delay. Marjorie Falis hurled bitter recriminations and a Ronson sterling lighter at her husband's back, calling him "Coward."

POETRY READING, poems spontaneously composed and recited (Aug. 27, 1966) by PETER PONZINI at home of OZZIE KLUTZ in Ptn., Mass.; readings were regular occasions for Ponzini to raise funds for his maintenance, with Klutz acting as host for friends and acquaintances; among those present were LAURENCE FAST, MARJORIE FALIS, BLACKY FALIS, TOM JONES, and SADIE MASSEY. Poems were composed orally and never written down by the author. Following is transcript of poems recited by Ponzini (lining transposed by breath groups):

> (title) *Truro.* A sky of clouds and winter held / The sea lay furrowed / Rose with the fields / Swept tall in dusk / We walked from hollows blind / To the east wind and the cry of gulls.
>
> (untitled). The dragger / Its port light / Red in the mean silence / Of the bay, / Nudges the channel buoy, / Steadies on the ebbing tide / To make fast / To the forsaken pier.
>
> (title) *Fall.* Like a wounded drake / The marsh bleeds in the thaw of crippled weeds; / Rusted and shaded / Gripped in the fist of the grey dawn /// Blind dawn, all dripping fall, / A frenzy of leaves lift on the cannon gusts / The mist enshrouds me, / It steams from bog and pot-hole; /// Rain weeps in the alders, / Boughs lean to the fog on languid elbows / Wet to its husk the earth like a sponge / Sucks up the sky in its thirst /// I hear the sea's grating / The clouds are winged buffaloes hoofed on the sea's echo / Armfuls of foam rise to the land crashing / The mussel-weeded drear and heedless rocks: /// I listen / I shall stand to the onrush of wind.
>
> (title) *Autumn, 1965.* It grips me unyielding / Yet alone / I favor milder times when time was an idea / Floating like a bubble from a child's pipe. /// In the year's slow turning, / In this mad sanctuary of miscalculation / The proud redeemer lifts a hand in recognition /// It grips me: / A freak in solitude, / Uncertain in my years / I turn the other cheek in stupefaction.

(title) *Genesis.* The complacent interval of time / Recedes like a roll of tin foil / into the wan evening: /// Eased of the world the butterfly / Rages indifferently against / The plot of radar. /// What of the raffish sparrow? a green blip / In the micro pulse of new despair? will it cling / With hooked claws to destiny? /// What of the worm in its rude habitat of earth / Shaken by ground waves that rip / The loose clutch of survival? /// Darwin makes concession to the toil / Of progress, abortive mutant in magnetic grace, / The fittest cry their outrage.

PONCHO (Araucanian, *pontho*), outer garment for protection against rain worn (July 26, 1966) by TOM JONES en route to home of BLACKY FALIS; poncho was draped over back of wicker chair from where it was brushed to the floor by the jacket sleeve of OZZIE KLUTZ at 9:30 p.m. At 2:30 a.m. (July 27), Hyman Hyman tripped over poncho on his way out of the Falis living room and suffered a broken leg.

PONZINI, PETER (PONZO) (1928–), Am. poet (oral trad.); spent youth in reformatories, Lattimer House (for the criminally insane) and the U.S. Army; no formal education. Noted with informal title as local poet in Ptn., Mass., where he has resided since 1954; poems are composed and recited spontaneously at various affairs during the "season" (June–Sept.). Employed during winter and spring as house painter, gardener for OSWALD KLUTZ, and fisherman. Gave dinner party (Aug. 17, 1966) at his residence on Shankpntr. Rd., at which a nine-pound STRIPED BASS was served to guests among whom numbered TOM JONES, SADIE MASSEY, LAU-

RENCE FAST, and BLACKY FALIS.

PROSTATE SPLINT, shown by PETER PONZINI to TOM JONES (July 15, 1966) in Ponzini's home on Shankpntr. Rd., Ptn., Mass. Ponzini told Jones that he had attached the splint one evening when having intercourse with a waitress from the Bonney Dune Rest. (Ptn., Mass.) Ponzini remarked about this: "I wanted to see what it would be like making it when I got old. I was in a very melancholy mood." When Jones asked how he (Ponzini) came to have such a thing in his possession, Ponzini replied that he had sent away for it. "I wanted to see what it would really be like when I got old," Ponzini said. Jones made the obligatory query and Ponzini answered, "Terrible."

PROVINCETOWN ART GALLERY POSTER ("Pictures to be read / Poetry to be seen"), on Bradford St., Ptn., Mass.; origin of a dialogue concerning the function of descriptive prose held (Aug. 3, 1966) between BLACKY FALIS and TOM JONES. Jones said the phrase "Poetry to be seen" confirms the value placed on writers who "make you see." Jones said, "Conrad makes you *see* the storm. Well, today, with no imaginative leap, no willing or unwilling suspension of disbelief, the same typhoon that Conrad saw is on your living room TV screen. Even a dolt who hadn't the attention span to read ten pages of the master can sit there awestruck as the *Narcissus* battles the elements. What virtue remains in page after page of the street, the mountain, the highway, the town, when a small team of professionals can make the same scene infinitely more real by really making you see it. Where are you going to take descriptive writing that Joyce or Proust left out? For a while the economics of movie-making will so limit the field that novels will be able to supply plots and subleties of thought that film can't touch, but for how long?" (Jones) Falis partially conceded Jones's point. He said, "The French and the Italians make the best movies and their novelists are better scenario writers than they are novelists." (See *VENUS AND ADONIS*.)

PROXIMA CENTAURI, 4½ light years from earth and nearest star; referred to in conversation (Aug. 9, 1966) by BLACKY FALIS; addressing an informal group at home of OSWALD KLUTZ in Ptn., Mass., Falis said he could envisage the day when America's rulers had destroyed the world, ". . . and when the boys are preparing that first escape rocket for Proxima Centauri, or wherever, you can bet who's going to be asked along. Up from the Virginia caves like maggots from a carcass they'll swarm into the waiting rocket." (Falis) (See *REVENGE OF THE CRYONOIDS*.)

PSYCHIATRIST'S VISIT, THE, visit paid (Sept. 2, 1966) to PETER PONZINI at his home on Shankpntr. Rd. in Ptn., Mass., by his former psychiatrist at the V.A. Psychiatric Clinic (NYC), Dr. E. Schroeder. Ponzini summoned his friends ALICE FAITH, LAURENCE FAST, BLACKY and MARJORIE FALIS, TOM JONES, SADIE MASSEY, and RUDI TREYF to view the pornographic films that Dr. Schroeder had brought with him. When they were assembled, Dr. Schroeder said, "I hate all the phony Christs dying for the people. He gives up of himself, Umph! An empty sac, a dry heave, Vat is there to give?

I tell you, a fish-eyed English-intellectual junkie-queen, so screwed up on his shtool like a corkscrew, shmoking his fag down to the end, like this, told me last night. The meteor flag of England shall yet terrific burn! Vell, shall ve dig the flicks? Let us dim the lights. Come, everyone." (Schroeder) Dr. Schroeder announced that the poor quality of the print they were about to see owed to the fact that it was a rare collector's item. He said that he had "many, many" films with him (Schroeder) and that he hoped to be able to show them all; he admonished every one to make himself comfortable. The guests smoked marijuana and hashish cigarettes while Ponzini prepared to screen a film entitled *Paris Nights* on his Bolex 18-5, 8 mm. movie projector. They were impatient with Dr. Schroeder's demeanor but anticipated with relish the automatic lust triggered by pornographic movies. During the screening of *Paris Nights* (Left Banke, 1929) a title conveyed the dialogue: "I know you prefer this . . . (scream), to that . . . (scream)." Marjorie Falis exclaimed, "O God, she's turning herself inside out," as the heroine writhed in agony at the end of a length of rope. As the title *The Aprodisiac Takes Effect* disappeared from the screen, Massey and Faith, as if by prearrangement, began to seductively caress their bodies and slowly remove their clothes. Marjorie Falis insisted that her husband escort her home. Treyf attempted to calm Falis but she shouted, "Psychoanalysts are repulsive!" (*See RAINY AFTERNOON*) and departed from Ponzini's. "Oh DO it! Marjorie," cried Massey, who stepped out of her panties and kicked them (with her sunburnt toe—Ed.) at the fleeing figure of M. Falis. After performing mutual cunnilingus, Faith and Massey had group intercourse with the men. B. Falis remarked to Treyf, "You're getting more than you bargained for, Sport, by not going home with Marjorie." "She asked *you* to take her home, Blacky," replied Treyf, kneeling between Alice Faith's sticky thighs. At 6:30 a.m. (Sept. 3, 1966) the leader of film of the last pornographic movie still turned on its reel. Everyone was asleep except Jones and Dr. Schroeder. "I don't understand it, we were all like humanoids," said Jones. Dr. Schroeder said, "I'm going back to NYC, I do believe I've had enough."

PURPLE DRESS, worn by VALERIE ANDERSON (Sept. 6, 1965) at her home on Wash. St., Hbkn., N.J.; in preparation for the arrival of her husband LANE who had promised to take her out for dinner in NYC; their boarder, TOM JONES, had agreed to baby-sit for the Andersons' child, Lee. Lane Anderson failed to appear and in her bitter disappointment, Valerie Anderson determined to enter into her first extramarital affair with Tom Jones. Later in the evening, when Jones and Anderson embraced, Jones put his hand underneath Anderson's purple dress. When they heard the front door close downstairs, they separated and listened to the footsteps on the stair. By the sound of the footsteps, Jones and Valerie Anderson were able to determine that Lane Anderson had come home drunk. (See *DAWN AT A HBKN. BALLFIELD.*)

R

RAINY AFTERNOON (July 26, 1966) in Ptn., Mass.; a group of friends including TOM JONES and SADIE MASSEY, BLACKY and MARJORIE FALIS, gathered at home of OZZIE KLUTZ; Dr. Rodney Fish, a prominent NYC psychiatrist, sat alone at a table drinking rye and sodas, beer, and smoking marijuana; occasionally he would take a handful of Ritilin tablets; Marjorie Falis became interested in his behavior and opened conversation with him by commenting on the poor weather. Dr. Fish said, "Ah, so you're the famous novelist's wife. How beautiful you are, my dear. The rage for beauty drives strong men insane and emboldens timid clerks. I know of a patient of Bill Kronkite who can't get an erection unless he is convinced that his partner is more beautiful than the one who preceded her. Women say they suffer beauty rather than enjoy it, that it's imposed on them by men. Some women today go so far as to insist that the major emphasis on a girl's good looks destroys the possibility of developing her intellect on par with a man's. Get that, her *intellect!* Rubbish. I get about two bitches a week lying down telling me they feel inferior to men, lying there pushing up their plump, juicy mounds. One I have to masturbate every week told me she didn't like to have intercourse with her husband when he was in a good mood, she liked to humiliate him first. And this one couldn't understand, poor booby, why it was always like *choking* (here

Dr. Fish grasped his throat with one hand) when she had to talk to her boss. Why I told her, Go down to the bars in the forties near the docks and pick 4 of the biggest Polacks, take them to some fleabag hotel and have intercourse with them. That'll get you over your fear around men. It's the active-intervention technique. It shortens duration of treatment. She'll be back Tuesday. That's how I get my kicks." (Dr. Fish) Later Marjorie Falis told her husband that Dr. Fish was "hideously depraved."

RAPE, subject of contest announced in *Strung-Out*, a London literary avant-garde magazine; read (June 11, 1966) by TOM JONES in his NYC apt.; Jones determined to enter the contest and win the £2,500 prize for the best piece of fiction received on the subject of rape. Following quotes his only attempt at writing for the contest, undated in ms.:

A Bit of Rape

It is usually impossible to get a desired position the first time in a rape. Complicated by struggle and malice, the initial entry can never be wholly satisfying. The best that can be hoped for is a resulting mood of submission and obedience attended by an increase in the sexual appetite. I might digress for a moment to criticize a popular superstition, namely that the woman in our culture is secretly a willing victim of assault. Like many misconceptions that enjoy a widespread currency, this one is rooted in a type of pseudo-fact. It is fair to say that many women are indeed anxious to be taken by force—however their conception of such violence is purely fantasy. Confronted by the shock of the real attack, the instinct toward self-preservation invariably takes the upper hand. (This can be no more than a spasmodic tightening in elderly victims.) It is precisely this instinct which must be triumphed over before the joys of abandon are allowed to govern. It is obvious that the woman who plays at rape with her lover or husband is not required to overcome the threat of injury or death. I cannot emphasize too greatly the importance of this primary obstacle, and its disintegration, to prepare the woman physically and psychologically for her role in the succeeding acts.

RAT STUDIES, which showed that marijuana decreased reproduction activity 90%; cited in conversation (Aug. 5, 1966) by BLACKY FALIS at his home in Ptn., Mass.; in conversation with MARJORIE FALIS, TOM JONES, SADIE MASSEY, and PETER PONZINI. Falis maintained that he had given up smoking marijuana for several reasons: His memory had been impaired, he often felt sluggish and without ambition, and he had sustained a chronic eye inflammation. He said he was unable to end his consumption of cigarettes, but had cut down radically. It was Falis's contention that when marijuana and LSD-25 were publicly accepted dangers, like cigarettes and automobiles, their sales would increase, thus confirming his well-known views of Am. cultural suicide (*See IMPARTIAL REVIEW*). Marjorie Falis said, "Horror-show theories, death urges, . . ." Her husband ordered her to be quiet, calling her a "drunken whore," and threatening her with violence if she couldn't keep still. On the other side, Tom Jones and Sadie Massey argued that the chronic users of marijuana and LSD-25, "the people" (Massey, in conversation), were already aware of the physiological changes that the drugs caused in their systems but in fact welcomed them as the necessary "physical-side" (Massey) to the changes they were experiencing "in their heads." (Massey) Massey pointed out that her views were in keeping with the overall theory of evolution. Jones went on to say that if the physiological and behavioral effects of the chronic usage of marijuana and LSD-25 were diagnosed clinically as schizophrenic, these "heads" (Jones) were prepared to inhabit clinical madness for their daily consciousness. Tom Jones said, "The willingness for everyone to be crazy at once expresses a great tolerance, absent in the culture even five years ago. People think if they're allowed to have their own freaky scenes whenever they want, then everyone else must be allowed to also." (*See DEANER-100.*)

RETURN OF THE VAMPIRE, THE, motion picture (Columbia, 1944, dir. Lew Landers) watched on TV (Aug. 27, 1965) by the ANDERSONS and TOM JONES, at the Anderson home on Wash. St., Hbkn., N.J.; they smoked hashish purchased earlier in the day from Paco Funes. (*See BUCKWHEAT BREAD.*) V. Anderson said, "I love the late-nite movies." L. Anderson expressed a preference for the vampire film over LES DYSTROPHES, which he and Jones had seen the previous day. He said, "It may not be art, but it's great with this hash." Jones said he imagined Bela Lugosi was a real vampire but had succumbed to Hollywood's wiles and become a heroin addict to avoid the "blood syndrome." V. Anderson replied that it was true that Bela Lugosi was a heroin addict.

REVENGE OF THE CRYONOIDS, composite science-fiction fantasy created (Aug. 6, 1966) by TOM JONES, BLACKY FALIS, and SADIE MASSEY, on Race Pt. Bch., Ptn., Mass.; Massey began by describing the new science of cryonics, which had been developed to freeze and preserve living tissue. Massey said, "It (cryonics) gets developed by renegades from established research projects whose work takes them too far along the dark road of man's presumption to govern himself completely. Human Conscience is offended, Frankenstein is in the air, the project is doomed." Falis continued the story, "That's when the Mafia appears secretly to the project leaders. 'We have need of such a device to insure the safety of our people,' whispers the hoarse voice of international malignancy, the genie in the machine. They provide the scientists with better facilities, a new plant, and the promise of becoming rich. Several in the top syndicate hierarchy, scheduled to appear before the grand jury, mysteriously vanish. The plan is to wait out the statute of limitations in cold storage, miles beneath the surface of the earth in secret caverns." At that point, Jones pursued the tale along another path: "After yrs. of intensive govt. investigation of the disappearances reveals nothing, a leak identifies one of the scientific crew on holiday in the Alps. Cryonics is deposited, again, within the public sector. This time it is better received. Annihilating forces crowd one another on the globe. Super-missiles poise twitching on every rocket site the world over." Whereupon

Falis resumed his version, "The American govt. decides to abandon earth to the forces of certain destruction and prepares to launch a fleet of spaceships with only the cream of the technocracy invited aboard. The rest, the rebels, outcasts, pariahs, misfits, are abandoned to their own schemes, to wit, cryonics. A freeze-in to save civilization takes place in the deserted govt. vaults, embedded deep within the rocky sphincter of Virginia. (See PROXIMA CENTAURI.) They set their thaw-timers to 20 yrs. and slam the lid. The world blows itself up, the American fleet is destroyed en route to the staging area, and the cryonoids creep out in 20 yrs. to inherit the earth." Massy inquired, "Why is it the 'Revenge of the Cryonoids'?" Falis replied, "Well, they survive, you see."

RITA METER MAID HANDBAGS, inspired by a song on the Beatles' lp. *Sgt. Pepper's Lonely Hearts Club Band* (Capitol) and sold (Oct., 1967) by TOM JONES through a national distributor. The item, priced at $5.95, created a sensation and made Jones rich and famous. The handbags were carried on a shoulder strap which gave them a military appearance; they were black, red, or green, and had the name "RITA" inscribed in white letters 3" high. (See HENRY JONES.)

ROACH, leftover butt of marijuana cigarette inserted (Sept. 11, 1966) into top of a Lark cigarette and smoked by TOM JONES and LAURENCE FAST in Jones apt. at 606 Comml. St., Ptn., Mass.; Jones who was distracted by his loss of SADIE MASSEY, told Fast of his feelings. Fast said, "She was a hip little chick, man, with a lot of ground to cover. You'd better forget about her and find yourself another." Tom Jones replied, "You'd have to understand how insecure she was." (*See* CURLY BLACK HAIR, SHE SAID SHE SAID, *and* TIFFANY.)

ROUND TABLE, in living room of JACOB LOWE's apt., 308 W. 73 St., NYC; where he received (Sept. 15, 1965) VALERIE ANDERSON and TOM JONES, who had come to seek Lowe's advice concerning their affair (*See* PURPLE DRESS *and* WE'RE OFF TO SEE THE WIZARD); they explained they were unable to decide what course of action to pursue, e.g., maintaining secrecy at the cost of their self-respect, or openly confronting LANE ANDERSON, at the risk of incalculable consequence. Lowe advised them to continue their affair in secret until they had decided upon a prearranged moment in which to spring the truth on Lane Anderson. Lowe prescribed this method in the light of his analytic knowledge of Anderson. He said in this way the infantile-masochistic gropings for self-pity would be short-circuited. Lowe made the analogy of himself as Merlin, L. Anderson as Arthur, Tom Jones ("our gallant young upstart," Lowe) as Launcelot, and V. Anderson as Guinevere. Tom Jones was disappointed in the obvious relish with which Lowe handled the situation. At an early point there was the following brisk exchange: Lowe (to V. Anderson): "Well, Valerie, does he fuck you any differently than Lane does?" Jones: "Oh, for Christ's sake, Jacob."

RUFUS, PLEASURES OF, THE, a pornographic novel published in Paris, Grope Press, 1944. Bound in green paper covers, 4½ x 7, 319 pp. Copy open to p. 6 (Aug. 18, 1966) on SADIE MASSEY's night table. TOM JONES saw it there at 11:30 a.m. He criticized Sadie Massey for spending the previous night with BLACKY FALIS. Page 6 reads as below:

The hashish had given me a fever; now the cocaine put me in a frenzy. In the next room the cat in heat screamed agonies of piercing loss; the strangulated seed, burning burning. I took my cock, purple and big in the red light, and pushed it into Jean. She opened like a deep wound. Back and forth, back and forth, until I couldn't stand it anymore. "Hurt me, hurt me," Jean begged. I withdrew completely from her. Her cunt was steaming and thick as honey. "Don't stop, don't stop," she moaned. "Why did you stop? it hurts me. Don't stop." I began to massage her clitoris slowly with my thumb and fingertips. "No, no"; Jean gagged for breath, her eyes were wild. "I want your cock inside me. I want you inside." I took her by her hips and turned her around fitting myself behind. Her thighs were hot and wet. It was sticky down to her knees. I took the dildo from the night table and before she knew what had happened, I had it in her to the hilt, turning it around, pushing it in, bringing it back almost to the tip. It drove her crazy. With one hard thrust I entered her ass and now I was fucking her completely. I could feel with my cock the deep thrusts of the dildo inside her pussy. I shot my load deep in her bowels. She buckled at the knees when she felt it coming; I didn't think I'd ever stop. She came a minute later, it was like a ball rolling slowly off a high table, the drop was sudden, deep and gone. I took out the dildo quickly, whipping it out. She looked outraged and angry, then she came one last time shrieking, struggling, clawing to escape the last costly descent. She closed her eyes and we both went to sleep. Her pussy made sounds like a percolator all night. (*See* HERSHEY.)

S

SALMON-PINK TABLECLOTH, freshly spread by MARJORIE FALIS (July 15, 1966) in preparation for an informal buffet at her home on Shankpntr. Rd., Ptn., Mass.; her guests included TOM JONES, SADIE MASSEY, RUDI TREYF, and a NY publisher. BLACKY FALIS entertained the company with remarks on the nation's "drug-ridden" youth. Falis commented, "The insane children sit hushed in decaying movie houses, their minds raped by speed and feedback, murderously exploited by their leaders, self-interested fanatics unfit for the struggle..." Jones interrupted to inquire whether Falis's remarks were meant to include JACOB LOWE as one of the leaders "unfit for the struggle." Falis said, "Lowe has led two generations down the drain with his odorless anarchism. (*See BEETHOVEN.*) Can you see him with a bomb in his hand? a little propaganda of the deed instead of all that insipid tolerance? No, it's all talk, always talk and useless demonstrations. There's no hope for him." (*See DAMAGED UPHOLSTERY.*)

SAWYER, EZEKIEL (ZEKE) (1931–), Am. chef and narcotics dealer, b. in Shreveport, La.; no formal education; married and left home while still in teens; served in U.S. Navy 1948–54; traveled with 2nd wife and two children to Los Angeles where he began to enlarge his narcotics operations. Several brief visits to Mexico during the period 1956–64. In 1965, experiencing harassment by local law-enforcement officials, Sawyer moved his family east to NYC. In the summer of that year he worked in Ptn., Mass., as head chef at the Inn of the Dunes. Introduced large quantities of LSD-25 into the Ptn. drug market. Returned to lucrative position during the following summer.

SCRIBE, brand of typewriter paper used (May–Sept., 1966) by BLACKY FALIS in Ptn., Mass. In the Falis study TOM JONES remarked (July 5, 1966), "You know, there are strange reports from all over about acid-babies being born with a third eye." Falis was amused and made a note on a piece of Scribe typing paper. He said, "The report I read speaks of chromosomatic damage and *mutant* babies." Jones replied, "I saw a child only 5 wks. old at the Balloon Farm (NYC) one night. His parents had taken acid when he was conceived and she had done a natural birth, taking only acid, and with her husband attended her. The baby was remarkably alert. Its eyes followed what was happening in the room. Then I saw them again at a party. It was very impressive. What I'm saying is that there will be a variety of mutants. A lot will depend on the genes of the parents." Falis objected, "That stinks like selective breeding."

SEX BURN, a psychosomatic condition so referred to by SADIE MASSEY (May 2, 1966); she described it to TOM JONES in NYC, as having the effect of "setting my skin on fire." She also said, "Sometimes any clothing at all, my bra or panties, makes such a friction on my nipples or the lips of my pussy, that I'm completely distracted until I can fuck." She added, "Once I was driving uptown from the East Side and I had a terrific sex burn in the car. I wanted to stop and have the first six guys who were there in the back seat. I was on the highway and there was a big jam-up. I couldn't get out of the car."

SHAFT OF LIGHT, thrown on the bed of room 39 at Inn of the Dunes Motel, Ptn., Mass. BLACKY FALIS and SADIE MASSEY were relaxing there after having sex (Aug. 28, 1966). "You look kind of sad," said Massey. Falis was silent. Massey added, "The light in this room is sad. A sad, gray afternoon in Provincetown." Falis said, "Every animal is sad after fucking except women and roosters." Massey asked, "What did you say to me?" Falis replied, "Triste est omne animal post coitum, praeter mulierem et gallumque. A Roman physician, Calennus." "Oh," exclaimed Massey, "did he know a lot about sex?" Falis said, "He knew that much."

SHE SAID SHE SAID, title of song (Lennon-McCartney, BMI) recorded by the Beatles on *Revolver*, Capitol Records; TOM JONES sat listening to this song (Sept. 7, 1966) and smoking marijuana in SADIE MASSEY's apt. at 381 Comml. St., Ptn., Mass.; Massey had left moments before on a sudden errand. She said she had acquired the new Beatles record and told Jones she would return in half an hour. Jones blamed BLACKY FALIS for giving Massey this new gift and supposed she had gone out to meet him. "She Said She Said" impressed Jones for reflecting the intense frustration of constant jealousy that he felt in his relationship with Massey. The line, "And you're making me feel like I've never been born," expressed this anxiety for him in a specifically appropriate way. He also felt that the nostalgia presented in the lines (beg.) "When I was a boy . . ." registered exactly the nostalgic warmth he was made to feel about his boyhood. (*See CURLY BLACK HAIR, ROACH, TIFFANY.*)

SHITTING A PUMPKIN, term used to describe childbirth by VALERIE ANDERSON (Oct. 28, 1965) in Hbkn., N.J., in conversation with TOM JONES; Jones had inquired, "What's it like to actually give birth?" LANE ANDERSON, who was present, added, "Yeah."

SHOPPING CART (metal basket on castors), in Singer's Supermarket (Nov. 7, 1965), Hbkn., N.J.; filled with groceries by VALERIE ANDERSON and TOM JONES, who took a box of Nabisco Mallomar cookies from the shelf and flipped it into the cart. Valerie Anderson read the label on the back of a can of Campbell's Cream of Asparagus Soup and said, "There's a recipe for a great sauce. I'll make a casserole for dinner. With mushrooms and artichokes." Tom Jones smiled and said, "Great," placing four cans of Snowcrop frozen orange juice concentrate into the cart. Valerie Anderson said, "Lane couldn't stand artichokes. Or mushrooms. All he wanted was meat and potatoes, chopped meat and mashed potatoes every night. He said it was because his teeth hurt him. Tom, do you think we'll be happy together?" Tom Jones took Valerie Anderson into his arms in an embrace as another shopping cart painfully crossed over his Achilles tendon. Several customers paused in their shopping to look at the couple with their arms wound around each other. The Muzac played, "Begin the Beguine." Valerie Anderson was crying softly.

"What about little Leezo?" she asked. Tom Jones said, "You know I adore Leezo." "But he'll miss his father," said Valerie Anderson sharply, drawing away. Tom Jones showed hurt in his face. "Will *you* miss him?" he asked, placing a box of Nabisco Socialite crackers in the shopping cart.

SILVER EARRINGS, worn by ALICE FAITH (Sept. 22, 1966) in the Foc'sle Bar in Ptn., Mass., where she sat drinking schooners of beer with LAURENCE FAST and TOM JONES. Fast admired her earrings. Faith said they came from Mexico. She said she was going to San Miguel de Allende, Guanajuato, in two weeks. She said she had a lift from NYC. Fast agreed to take Faith into NYC when he drove there to begin working in ten days. Jones told Faith that he had visited S.M.A. for a few weeks in 1962. He said that Faith ought to enjoy herself in Mexico. "You can get junk over the counter in drugstores there," Jones told her (Faith). (*See AKTEDRON.*)

SNIDE, KARL (1915–), Am. writer and social critic; graduated Wisc. Univ., 1934, M.A.; earned reputation in mid-thirties for trenchant criticisms of Am. life; worked as film critic for *Time Magazine* in 1940s; contributing editor of IMPARTIAL REVIEW, 1950–55; literary mentor of EUGENE ANGRIE and others. His books include *Make It Now, Becoming of Now,* and *The Palace of Now.* Gave following verbal report (Oct. 24, 1958) to a police officer investigating a disturbance in the San Remo Bar in NYC: "He (CHARLES "BLACKY" FALIS) came right into the bar where we (Snide and Eugene Angrie) were standing. His (Blacky Falis) first words were, 'I hear you shot me down, sport.' BF (Blacky Falis) looked very mean. Eugene said, 'Not at all, Blacky, I really dig you.' There was a flash of something in BF's face and I thought he was going to swing on Eugene. But he didn't. Instead he yelled, 'You don't even know me, man.' Right in Eugene's face. Eugene said, 'Take it easy, take it easy.' BF backed down for a second, then he really got mad and said, 'You son of a bitch, who told you that story about the squash? Who told you?' Eugene said, 'Nobody told me anything. I made it all up.' Then BF hit him twice very quickly in the face. When Eugene got up his glasses were broken and his lips were bleeding. He said, 'You shoulda sued, you bastard. Now I'm going to sue the hell out of you.' That's all, officer. BF stood around for a moment, then he left." (*See* SQUASH.)

SPERM WHALE (spermaceti whale; *Physeter catodon*), discovered dead (July 22, 1966) on a beach between N. Truro and Ptn., Mass. PETER PONZINI, ALICE FAITH, and TOM JONES were among those who drove in Ponzini's beach jeep from the Foc'sle Bar in Ptn. to the site on the beach where the whale washed up. Ponzini climbed to the top of the whale's head and spontaneously wrote and recited a poem on the "majesty of the great fish which the sea will reclaim." (Ponzini) Faith asked Jones whether he had been to Europe, particularly Greece or Italy. Jones was on the verge of response when Ponzini interrupted his eulogy to shout at Alice Faith, "Don't go to Italy. All they want to do is shine your shoes and sell you chewing gum. Stay here on the Cape where you can live in nature."

SQUASH, type commonly known as winter squash (*Cucurbita maxima*); half of such a squash, baked with honey and raisins, was served to Hildegaard Falis at a birthday dinner prepared for her by her husband, BLACKY FALIS. (June 20, 1953), in their apt. at 336 Central Pk. W., NYC. Also invited were EDGAR and AMY COOPER. When squash was served to Hildegaard Falis she said, "But Blacky, I don't eat squash." Blacky Falis, who was inebriated, replied, "Well, madam, I missed my guess on the squash, but how would you enjoy a piece of my cock?"

STANZAS FOR THE SEDER, poem written by TOM JONES; work on the poem was begun May 19, 1966, and concluded on the afternoon of May 21, 1966. (*See BEADED NECKLACE.*) Text of poem, follows below:

Stanzas for the Seder

   Why is tonight different?
I am alone and still in bondage;
My people celebrate their bitter dinners
And have no place to go.

Suppose one, on that last night choking
In the desert, passed in shadows through the camp
Leaving the stench and the sentries' desperate rim,
Read in the stars and in the wind the cold lesson
Blown across the Polish marshes, the stagnant ponds
Where his sons would go swimming in a sack
With a dog and a snake and a rat,
Saw then the shambles of the myth, the bearded
Lies, and with the dawn boiling in his ears
Walked sadly back to Egypt.

STRAIGHT LEFT JAB

> Why is tonight different?
> I am alone and still in bondage;
> My people flourish in the promised land
> And have no place to go.

STRAIGHT LEFT JAB, (landed Sept. 23, 1965) on face of Hbkn. bar-girl by unidentified man wearing a blue denim work shirt. This action was a prelude to further violence in the Triangle Bar, a rowdy meeting place on River St. TOM JONES and LARRY EARLY were seated on stools at the bar when the fighting broke out. They were unable to remove themselves to a safer place as the melee went on in front of them blocking the exit. The man who had struck the girl, knocking her from her stool, was attacked by four other men. The fight went on for eleven minutes with the man in the denim work shirt alternately receiving and dealing the greatest punishment. At one point he received help from a gray-haired man. Together they held down one of their attackers and drove the heels of their shoes into his face and groin. The most serious injury was sustained by one of the combatants who was beaten simultaneously on the head by two police officers with clubs. The police were summoned by the bartender, PETER KAZANOVSKY. Jones and Early were astonished by the bloodshed and Jones experienced a weakness in his knees afterward as he and Early walked out of the Triangle Bar.

STREET SINGER, a person of indeterminate identity dressed in shabby harlequin costume; appeared (morning, May 10, 1966) in the interior courtyard beneath the windows of TOM JONES's apt. at 1265 Second Ave., NYC; serenaded tenants of adjacent buildings with song; accompanied himself on mouth organ and accordion. SADIE MASSEY and Tom Jones leaned out of the kitchen window and applauded loudly after each song. Sadie Massey said, "I've never seen anything like this, ever." Tom Jones said, "Either have I." Tom Jones disappeared from the window and returned with a sock filled with pennies which he threw down. Other tenants threw loose change. After the street singer had gone Tom Jones said, "This is going to be a great day. Let's go rowing in Central Park." Sadie Massey replied, "It's not warm enough, let's get out of New York." (*See BOX OF KLEENEX and DICED CHICKEN WITH ALMONDS.*)

STRIPED BASS (*Roccus saxatilis*), 9 lbs., caught by PETER PONZINI (Aug. 17, 1966) and served that night to his guests for dinner; as TOM JONES was enjoying a second helping, SADIE MASSEY said, "BLACKY FALIS has been coming on to me all summer. I'm going to sleep with him tonight." Tom Jones asked, "Is that why you moved out? So you could sleep around?" Sadie Massey replied, "I am above replying to your vulgarity. If you loved me you wouldn't say things like that." Tom Jones said, "I do love you. The more I love you the more you torment me. I don't think you're wicked. It's the LAW OF DIMINISHING RETURNS." "You overintellectualize everything," said Sadie Massey. Tom Jones came upon a bone in a mouthful of fish. "What an ugly look," exclaimed Sadie Massey. (*See PENNY.*)

T

TENDERNESS, shown (Aug. 4, 1966) by BLACKY FALIS toward his wife MARJORIE; in the shower in their home, Ptn., Mass.; as Falis soaped up his wife's body he felt a glowing compassion toward her, though he admitted to himself never being in love with her. Actually he thought her vulgar, but strongly admired her independence and vitality. He recalled a period during which his wife had never failed to erotically arouse him by the slightest contact, but this had passed within a few months. He considered that in every way except that in which his present wife experienced orgasm, she was a better mate for him than his first wife, Hildegaard, had been. (*See WATER-SKIING.*)

THC (tetrahydrocannabinol), the active ingredient in marijuana; cited in conversation (July 28, 1966) by TOM JONES in the Cellar Bar in Ptn., Mass. Jones told LAURENCE FAST that research was nearly completed on a synthetic form of marijuana using THC, which could be marketed legally under existing legislation. Fast replied that it was his opinion that the drug could never be legal. "There are too many important people making money off it being illegal, man." (Fast)

THREE BOILED POTATOES, on the plate of TOM JONES (Nov. 2, 1965) at the Anderson home at 306 Wash. St., Hbkn., N.J.; Tom Jones, friend and upstairs tenant, was a dinner guest of the Andersons. The boiled potatoes had just been speared by Tom Jones from a large oval dish containing many potatoes. LANE ANDERSON, touching a corner of his napkin to his lips, said, "Valerie, have you been sleeping with Tom?" VALERIE ANDERSON said, "Yes, but I love him." Lane Anderson said, "Oh, my God." And then loudly sobbed. "Oh God," sprawling across his plate of ham, cabbage, and boiled potatoes. (*See GRASSY KNOLL.*)

TIFFANY (1964–), Am. domestic cat (*Felis domesticus*), white with black markings, owned by SADIE MASSEY. Sadie Massey and TOM JONES were seated (Sept. 6, 1966) in her apt. at 381 Comml. St., Ptn., Mass. Sadie Massey served jasmine tea which was a favorite with Jones. She said, "I'm leaving with Blacky in two days. Maybe Spain. Nobody knows about it. But I want to ask you a favor. I want you to take care of Tiffany for me. I couldn't bear to think of anyone else having her. You will, Tom love, won't you?" Tom Jones replied, "God, Sadie, I hope you know what you're doing. You must know how I love you. How can you leave me now? After all we've had together." Sadie Massey said, "Oh, Tom, nothing is forever. Please keep Tiffany." She kissed him on the mouth. Tom Jones became emotional and pushed his face against Sadie Massey's breasts. "Yes," he said, "yes, I will." Two weeks later Tom Jones returned from a walk and discovered that Tiffany had given birth to six kittens on his bed. The afterbirth gave off a terrific odor. He sat down in his living room and lit a cigarette. "Damn," he said aloud. "I will never be free of that girl." (*See CURLY BLACK HAIR, ROACH, and SHE SAID SHE SAID.*)

TOAST, proposed (Aug. 9, 1965) in The Triangle Bar, Hbkn., N.J., by LANE ANDERSON; Anderson proposed toast to TOM JONES after he and Jones had spent the previous evening (Aug. 8) drinking in the bars in NYC. Anderson and Jones returned to N.J. because of the 4 a.m. NYC closing regulations; bars in Hbkn. open at 5:30 a.m. They spent the "dead hour" (Anderson) in the Town Lunch, Hbkn., before PETEY KAZANOVSKY served them their first beer at 5:33 a.m. Following is verbatim account of Anderson's toast: "Let's drink a toast to all the chronic masturbators. To all those who cannot leave it off, to all those that must have their shame in their enjoyment. To those waiting for their girl friend to come home, one hand reading a comic the other jerking off, in subways, bars, and public toilets, amusement parks, elevators and movie theaters, in museums, bus terminals, and Eng. Dept. offices, to him who has trouble with his fly, to all self-sufficient, loony, miserable Masturbators."

TOILET CHAIN, used by TOM JONES (June 13, 1966) as a figure of speech to describe the smashed arm of a girl who had jumped from a fourth-floor window at ELEVEN WEST HUDSON ST., NYC. Jones said, "I used to work in an ambulance collecting people for Roosevelt Hospital (NYC)." Jones and SADIE MASSEY had been the first to arrive in the street and Jones had attempted to discover the extent of the girl's injuries. His actual words were: "Her arm's broken in a thousand places. It's like picking up a toilet chain."

TOM'S DREAM, on the night of April 11, 1966, in his apt. at 1265 Second Ave., NYC. Jones was in bed asleep with SADIE

MASSEY when he awakened with a scream. He described his nightmare to Massey, who attempted to soothe him. He said he had been dreaming of shaking hands with a man whose face he couldn't remember when the skin on the man's hand began to crawl onto Jones's. The skin turned into a mass of crabs, or pubic lice. Jones awoke in horror. Sadie Massey said, "Poor Tom. I probably shouldn't have told you. We'll go to the doctor tomorrow." Jones replied, "It doesn't matter. It's only a bad dream." (*See GLOM, ADOLF, DR., and GIMMIE, EDWARD.*)

TREYF, RUDI (1932–), Polish-Am. artist, b. Cracow, son of wealthy industrialist; educated mainly in France and USA, degrees from Sorbonne and Yale Univ.; prolific exponent of multi-media constructions, panels; opts for scientific language "without irony" (Jules Bulard, *Art News*, 1966). Treyf visited Ptn., Mass. (June–Sept., 1966) as guest of OSWALD KLUTZ; his diptych, HELLO TO YOU, attracted much attention in Ptn. art circles; entered affair with MARJORIE FALIS. Treyf returned to teaching post at Yale Univ. in fall of 1966.

TROIS MORCEAUX EN FORME DE POIRE, piano composition by Erik Satie (1886–1925) recorded on Angel Records (35442); disc released by spindle on TOM JONES's RCA phonograph (March 12, 1966) in his apt at 1265 2nd Ave., NYC, at the moment Jones and SADIE MASSEY concluded having sexual intercourse for the first time. Massey said, "I hope you don't like me less for going to bed with you the first day I met you. I think it's the only honest thing to do if you like someone." Jones replied, "I think you're just a love, Sadie." (See

YOU CAN LEAD A WHORE TO CURIOUS, ETC.)

TWENTY-SIX JANE STREET, APT. 5-F., apt. in NYC where TOM JONES and SADIE MASSEY attended a party (May 9, 1966); entire apt., including floor, ceilings, furnishings, and kitchen equipment (range, refrigerator, sink, etc.) was painted bright red and lighted by green light bulbs. When Jones and Massey entered they were greeted by their host, Adam Mullaney, who wore only red trousers and red suspenders. The other guests were smoking marijuana in a large water pipe placed in the middle of the floor. Tom Jones and Sadie Massey found space to sit at the end of the living-room couch and waited for their turn with the pipe.

TWO SPANISH PLAYS, referred to and described (Aug. 25, 1966) by TOM JONES to PETER PONZINI, in Ponzini's home on Shankpntr. Rd., Ptn., Mass.; Ponzini discussed the applied discipline of some Zen monks who exchange the role of man for beast as an instructional guidance. "These men live just like beasts, sometimes for years," Ponzini said. Jones related the plot of Calderon's *La Vida Es Sueño*, and then told Ponzini that he had been reminded of another Spanish play which dealt with a man approached by the devil at a time in his life when his business was failing and his mistress was about to desert him. The devil offered to restore his business and his mistress's affection if the man agreed to sign a paper giving the devil the right to the life of an anonymous person in China, who would die as the ink dried on the contract. The man agreed to the devil's bargain, the reversals in his career abruptly ended and were put right, and at that point,

Jones admitted, his accurate recollection of the plot was curtailed. However, he felt strongly that the play continues with the Spanish businessman somehow confronting the widow or close relative of the person (or a person) who has recently died in China. Jones remembered that the encounter took place on a rowboat, but could not recall the connecting narrative. Jones related how the man is convinced that the person in the rowboat with him is mourning the soul whose fate he had signed away to the devil. Finally the man's conscience forces him to release the soul he had bargained over and consign his own soul to the devil. "Which was what the devil was after from the beginning, which was why he came to the Spanish businessman and not the man in China." (Jones)

U

UNMATCHING BOOTS (PAIR), one brown and one red, worn (July 16, 1966) by Neal Cassady in Ptn., Mass., in company of TOM JONES and SADIE MASSEY, at their apt., 606 Comml. St.; joined by PETER PONZINI, they smoked marijuana and listened to jazz records. Cassady complained that his name was often misspelled in print, he said, "N-e-a-l C-a-double-s, although his father wrote it the other way and his later records so attest it is an 'a'—my climb—the true mind of the true Jewish mother that knows that the sexiest redhead . . . ah, I really do know a cat, who—, just a head, about thirty, he did five to life for the same thing I did, not for 1st-degree armed robbery you know, for all *they* knew, yeah, so he said, 'I wonder what it's like?' So *she* came home at 3:30 and he was in San Quentin. The eye confirms the hand? Then don't just fiddle around with anything. An order is in effect until fulfilled, superseded, or annulled. Why didn't you finish the film, Kesey? they asked. He's carrying this bag, he edited it, too. I purposely disentangled you to entangle you. Well, Audie Murphy went on with his killing, isn't he too much? Finally got shot in the heel . . . He never exhales, says Tom Wolfey the 2nd, to think, let alone to breathe, as we all are. We all *Are*? Where was that apache, dear? We've had too many Alastair Sims in our boudoir before. Which bedroom are we in today? . . . I killed my own leaders under taboo, what should we do? I've been a prince too, in Bedouin times and saw my gangster tradition violated much as the Indians 100 yrs. ago were violated and are today. Is violation the way? Well, there was no hope in those guys' eyes 3 yrs. ago, as much as there *was* hope in some other guys' eyes. Christ was just a man before he was Christ, Jesus was, of course, only a man, historically, like at 30 Mohammed became a prophet, Ah-men, said the old maid under the bed . . . Nobody knew when it was going to happen. Kerouac wrote a science fiction novel, you know, all about just suddenly you weren't, 'Who's this, you?' 'Not me, man, I just . . .' Karma, if you refuse to meet the conditions, the terrain forces . . . (Cass got trapped in his own damn Cass) only I'm a writer, no fuck Cass. To Cayce, no Kesey, to make it easy, as Arnie misses his putt—not knowing a thing—I'm not a doctor and so can't begin. New Knowledge from Without—You can't register yourself cleanly enough ever evereverevever. What key is ever in? . . . He said, 'You're Moriarity?' He gave me a per for 30 amphetamine at a party . . . She doesn't have to replay, then, my football games in gravel or anything-I-chose-not-to-replay myself to remember getting a football out of in the 9th grade, I turned 10, of course, the next. Well, football is all there is men, so win one for the Gipper! You know, we all go off the walls with Karachicla who always wore knee cupies. This girl was always rubbing my testes, but I didn't let it go, so there you are. What is it? What I'm catching from you, seeking to externalize, escape from no identity-individually-like me. If you dig a hole, fill it up . . . 60 days said the judge to me. I said, 'Huh?' I said, 'Yeah, judge, 38 months living off my friends. Every night's been New Year's Eve. Think of that.' And Ferlinghetti rhymes with confetti.—I'd be talkin' to all the heads in the audience. They'd all be zonked and that meant *everything* to them. Everything to them. (I'll say it again, you prick. Shut up, Cass, you ought to lose your teeth.) . . . Is that a fact? Subliminally expressed to his drink-sodden, dope-ridden no ridd-opened. Well, he had hopes there, just a couple . . . You American man, who stands! (addressed to Peter Ponzini) Most Am. men wish they didn't have to. Who wants to catch a train at 6 a.m. in the cold latitudes? Do not, Miss Murphy, mistake kindness for weakness. The negative always destroys itself.—I read too many books when I was a kid—what time is it again, Coxswain? I'm at the helm—I started to join instantly but he said, 'Don't be a nut kid, you'll be dead.' As it turned out to be, a few others agreed. Thank goodness some shipmates are forced on us . . . Everything's true on every level at once, though. But if you're actually spiritually unfolding, that which in the mind of the object is timewise enduring—like to the eye of the cat the house walks by—It's hard enough to actualize physically, you see, instead of violate . . . I can remember, I did, I went 1 min. 22 secs. without thinking of myself. The other night. Try it—That was the record, I think it was held . . . I beat her though, the girl who *didn't* think of herself. She was kind of a slow type, no she was a fast one.—Well, a younger girl. . . . Confined to the rigors of the N. American continent, the black man begins to say Fuck this Shit, Dad—Burroughs, the greatest thing in the century thinks Kesey, the greatest novelist since W.W. II. Kesey never did more than agree with anything—

as every moment in time we all do with each other's minds. Then again, some mornin's I'd rather not—Now who's foolin' who, Cass? You're dead. Hello, out there, I'm dead. Hello, in there, I'm dead. Just a gigolo, dead. The world goes on around me instead of barbiturates. 'Boxcars'll still be there, kid,' they said. I said, 'What's binders?' He said brakes. I know what I'm talking about, honestly." (Cassady)

U.S. AIR FORCE FLIGHT JACKET, worn by SADIE MASSEY (July 21, 1966) in the evening; she was walking on Race Pt. Bch. with TOM JONES, who put his arm around her. Jones said, "You feel great in this jacket." Massey said, "Wow, look at the ocean." They stood in silence and watch the sea until they became chilly.

V

VEGETABLE, metaphor, used to describe SADIE MASSEY by her father, Ivan, over telephone (June 23, 1966) in BEACON HOTEL, NYC; Massey told TOM JONES, when he returned with cigarettes from the hotel pharmacy, that she had been disturbed by a telephone conversation with her parents while he was out. She was particularly upset by her father's remark that she had become a vegetable. She immediately began to write in her notebook and alternately brooded and wrote for several hours in a chair by the window. Later in the day she showed her notebook to Jones. (Text follows below:)

> Did someone forget to tell me something I'm supposed to know? Now I hear people call me a vegetable—can you imagine? A cabbage. I turned my first four leaves out and bid him hello. . . . We choose our moments-we do not-We make our own bed-we do not-We think-knowing nothing would pass by chance-We pursue an illusion-We personify our fool-we do not pursue-We personify our fool-to the right-to the left-we plug-we turn-replug-to learn to unplug-replug unlearn. . . .
>
> Are you really happy? asked a girl. Only when I'm not sad thought I. . . .
>
> Suddenly the world is so much smaller than a pinpoint. Can everyone read one another's mind? Is it fact

or paranoia? People talk in several voices, telling me they're mad. Have I ended up an observer of the mad? I must not stop along the way to extend a helping hand. What for? . . .

Good morning! I had a friend with colored shampoo! It was so *rich* it made my head flow like rainbows!

Van: "They took everything I had."

David: "I don't care if I write anymore."

To have the life's blood sucked out of you. To have the mantis pray over your body. To crash like a moth into the fire. To have your wings burned. To have your face "taken." To be forced to sell, to hurt, to fear encouraging yourself because Are your dreams worth it? And no one will tell you, and even if they do, how can you believe them? . . .

How can you *love* on earth if you know you must give it up? The only limits are the ones you believe in. Is to value the same as to limit? What is there to value, only the moment. . . . CASE 45—from *The Book of Karma Points*.

Perry: He has finally stopped drooling profusely when we permit him the pleasure of play and proceeds in the usual manner. His craft seems to be heightening—he almost responds when he succeeds in prodding the insects to battle. A curious aspect has developed on which I might ask advice. He has taken to twitch the r. side of his face as each meal is served, muttering about the salt in the air. Perhaps cook is using too much salt. I must look into this.

VENUS AND ADONIS, poem by Shakespeare, in which JACOB LOWE noticed (Sept. 8, 1965) the word "bare" (l. 188) as his eye fell across the page turning to another poem. The usage was unexceptional in every way, which was the point that attracted Lowe. He conjectured that such phrases as "bare excuses" and a "bare tale," emerging from a culture in which men were concerned about clothing and shelter, were doomed by the technology of the modern culture. As a writer he was not discouraged by the impending impotence of language, but was stimulated by the state of flux. He believed in McLuhan's vanguard of tribal role-players and considered the language had been enriched by the lively argot borrowed from technology. He saw herds of young people "putting on" costumes to play a role, while they "put on" their fathers who wore suits to go to their jobs. Then came to mind lines of poetry Lowe could not identify, "His thoughts are so much higher than his state, / That like a mountain hanging o'er a hut, / They chill and darken it." (*See PROVINCETOWN GALLERY POSTER.*)

VIETNAM (U.S. WAR IN), referred to, in passing aside (Aug. 17, 1966) by BLACKY FALIS at home of PETER PONZINI in Ptn., Mass.; Falis was speaking to a group of friends, including Ponzini, TOM JONES, and SADIE MASSEY, when he said, "Vietnam? All of you know what I think about Vietnam, but did you know they're giving the combat troops a 90-day early discharge if they join a police force back home?" Asked by Massey whether he (Falis) thought that the conflict in Vietnam would precipitate World War III, he replied, "Yeah, probably." (See *FUCKED IN THE ASS*.)

VOLUME CONTROL, adjusted to low, by SADIE MASSEY (July 28, 1966) on PETER PONZINI's Voice of Music phonograph, in Ponzini's home, Shankpntr. Rd., Ptn., Mass.; Massey complained she was unable to hear what Ponzini was saying. BLACKY FALIS agreed with her that the Bessie Smith recording (CL 538) was playing too loudly to support conversation. Ponzini repeated that, in his opinion, Allen Ginsberg was "no kind of poet." (Ponzini) When Massey took strong exception to this remark, Ponzini demanded proof of Ginsberg's poetic credentials. Massey declared passionately, "I know Allen's a poet because he shoveled corpses into the Ganges, baby. What other kind of proof do you need?" Falis criticized Massey's argument saying that such experience in itself wasn't evidence of any poetic qualities in Ginsberg's writing. Massey explained, "Well, to hell with both of you, then. Go back and read his poems some more."; she rose swiftly and made her way out of the house, calling "Later" behind her when she reached the door to the street. Ponzini adjusted the volume control to high, saying, "I'd like to fuck her little bun off, boil her panties and make a chowder." Falis saw Ponzini's lips moving but could not distinguish his words. "What?" yelled Falis.

W

WALL POSTERS (CHINESE), used in conversation (April 19, 1965) by TOM JONES to express a "cultural metaphor" (Jones); with LANE ANDERSON in the Anderson home at 307 Wash. St., Hbkn., N.J. Jones maintained that the same relationships held true in a cultural way for the Chinese Red Guards and their wall posters, as for "the American kids and their rock music." (Jones) "This is the language the best kids in both countries are using to express themselves. In both cultures these forms are immensely popular, yet officially frowned on. And although everyone today reads the wall posters and listens to rock music, I think it is intentional that the creative value remains with the kids." Anderson agreed and added, "They both speak in languages I don't understand." (*See LOOP OF HAIR.*)

WATER-SKIING, an aquatic sport engaged in by BLACKY FALIS and his wife, MARJORIE (July 22, 1966) in Ptn., Mass.; as Falis piloted his small, fiberglass boat, taking care to keep watch on his wife trailing behind on the skis, he felt a remarkable tenderness toward her and saw in her smile a reciprocal feeling. Later he reflected that his feeling had been inseparable from the technology involved in maintaining several systems (the speed and direction of the boat, the slack of the line, his wife's speed and direction) simultaneously. (*See TENDERNESS.*)

WEDDING BAND, GOLD, worn by VALERIE ANDERSON and removed by her (Sept. 29, 1965) before going to bed with TOM JONES in Hbkn., N.J. Valerie Anderson had requested that she and Jones make love in his upstair apt., rather than in the downstairs bedroom she shared with her husband, LANE. When Jones discovered that Anderson had removed her wedding band, he asked, "Why did you take this off?" Anderson replied, "You shouldn't be so sensitive, Tom."

WEDGWOOD ASHTRAY, overturned by TOM JONES (Feb. 22, 1966) in his apt. at 1265 2nd Ave., NYC; Jones was startled by the ringing of his telephone, which had been disconnected for failure to pay his bill in Nov., 1965. He was seated in his living-room armchair and experiencing the diminishing effects of 450 mcg. of LSD. When Jones picked up the receiver, he heard an operator inquiring whether he would be home in the morning, as a workman was being dispatched to remove the phone from his apt.

WE'RE OFF TO SEE THE WIZARD, pop. song from Walt Disney's *Wizard of Oz;* sung on Hudson Tubes (Trans-Hudson underwater subway) by VALERIE ANDERSON and TOM JONES (Sept. 15, 1965) on their way to visit JACOB LOWE (*See* ROUND TABLE) in quest of advice concerning their affair. V. Anderson told Jones, when they had finished singing, "I'm sure Jacob will think of the best solution to all this. I can't keep it a secret from LANE (ANDERSON) much longer. I get stiff whenever he wants to touch me." Tom Jones shifted uncomfortably in his seat. "You could smoke some hashish when you're in bed," he said.

WET SOUNDS, heard by TOM JONES (Aug. 11, 1965) as he gained consciousness after passing out in the ANDERSON living room; sounds were directed from the Anderson bedroom. Jones sat up in the armchair and listened. He could also hear low voices. Jones had taken supper with the Andersons and afterward sat in the living room drinking beer and smoking marijuana. After listening to the Andersons have intercourse, Jones went upstairs to his bedroom and masturbated.

WHO ARE THE HOTENTOTS?, question asked (April 14, 1965) by VALERIE ANDERSON of TOM JONES, who had stated, "LANE (ANDERSON) said JACOB (LOWE) was addressing the Hotentots tonight in Washington." (*See NAVY WORK SHIRT.*) L. Anderson, wearing his new shirt and drinking a can of Schlitz beer, said, "Hotentots are African bushmen." The Andersons and Jones expressed their great admiration for Lowe. "For all his personal faults he is a great man," said V. Anderson. "I wish he weren't such a prick to his putative friends," replied L. Anderson. V. Anderson inquired the meaning of the word "putative." Jones supplied the meaning. L. Anderson entered a private reverie while V. Anderson and Jones discussed Dostoevski's *The Idiot*, which V. Anderson had just finished reading. "I was crying when I heard you and Lane come up the stairs," she said. L. Anderson abruptly said, "This Schlitz beer gives me a skin rash," and lapsed again into silence.

WHY IS EVERYONE SO CRAZY? question raised and answered (Aug. 21, 1966) by TOM JONES in Ptn., Mass.; Jones addressed himself to SADIE MASSEY, LAURENCE FAST, ALICE FAITH, and

ZEKE SAWYER; Jones said he had perceived, while listening to a Bob Dylan record on the phonograph, that the sibilant S's whispered conspiracy. He said the idea of a secret society was impossible to ignore; he suggested that only a certain type of understanding would make the connections necessary to "dig where Dylan's lyrics are at." (Jones) The amazing fact was, he said, that this music was immensely popular. "And yet when you think of where most people's heads are still at, you understand that it's as if a whole piece of continent just broke off and drifted out to sea. That's why whenever you deal with 'proper society' it's impossible to avoid inventing a double self to keep your secret safe. Which is schizophrenia. That's why everyone is so crazy." (Tom Jones) (*See* BURNT PIECE OF DRIFTWOOD *and* CIGARETTE ASH.)

WOOL SWEATER (GREEN), patched by VALERIE ANDERSON (Oct. 6, 1965) at her home on Wash. St., Hbkn., N.J.; TOM JONES sat in the living room with her, drinking a cup of coffee. LANE ANDERSON had gone shopping for dinner at the Hbkn. Pork Store on the corner. Valerie Anderson asked Jones whether or not he thought she should allow Leezo (the Anderson child, Lee) to own a puppy. She added that Emily Lowe had told her that puppies eat cushions and shoes. She complained that Leezo wasn't getting on properly with the other children his age (4 yrs.). She said he was always falling down and ripping his clothing. She said she had repaired the green sweater twice in the past two weeks. She wanted to know whether Tom Jones thought that Leezo was "accident prone." She told him that she had read an article in a magazine which said some children "just are." (V. Anderson) Valerie Anderson went on to say that at lunchtime she had allowed the sink to congest with food particles; she said it took 2½ hrs. before the drain would operate properly.

Y

YOU CAN LEAD A WHORE TO CURIOUS BUT YOU CAN'T MAKE HER THINK, saying devised (March 12, 1966) by SADIE MASSEY, during an evening spent with TOM JONES in his apt. at 1265 2nd Ave., NYC. (*See TROIS MORCEAUX EN FORME DE POIRE.*)

YOUTHFUL EXHIBITIONIST, on Race Pt. Bch., Ptn., Mass., who accidentally extracted (June 29, 1966) his upper and lower front teeth attempting to open a Coca-Cola bottle; passed by TOM JONES without notice as he walked along the beach mentally composing a poem. Jones walked to 606 Comml. St. where he wrote the words of the poem in a loose-leaf binder belonging to SADIE MASSEY. (Following quotes text of poem:)

> After the Storm (title)
>
> The short grass swims in its own juice,
> puddles and pools,
> I think of rice-paddies and a body
> bobbing like a cork in swill . . .
> a thin edge of nostalgia intervenes,
> how the streets looked in the capital,
> every afternoon it rained at four,
> metal shuttered storefronts slammed shut,

as we scurried by, each one glistening
in his cheap, plastic sheet . . .

The darkened t.v. tube reflects the bay,
sparrows flutter and a gull turns,
a sudden wind striates the sky like a test-pattern;
last night the tube gleamed blue
as the nation's villains, ape-necked,
heckled our failing conscience for more death,
their determination streaming like electrons
through every pore—I could not shut it out;
only the storm refused to witness, gaily
striking the antenna from my captive roof . . .

Z

ZOO CAFETERIA (NYC), in Central Park, where TOM JONES and SADIE MASSEY met for lunch (May 11, 1966); they sat outside at a table with sun awning. Jones told Massey that, seated at the same table two years earlier, he had written a play. He described the play as a Shavian dialogue in one act between a leonine young man, who claimed he was sired by a lion in Africa (to his missionary mother's chagrin and dismay) and a girl whose acquaintance he was trying to make. They discuss whether it is edifying or cruel to keep wild animals in zoos. Sadie Massey giggled and said, "You're very clever, Tom." Jones puffed with pride.

About the Author

Richard Horn was born on December 18, 1942, in New York City, the only child of Howard Horn, a proprietor in the textile industry (according to the 1950 U.S. Census), and Evelyn Horn, a Russian immigrant and former shopgirl in a midwestern department store who eventually rose to become vice president of the chain. Horn was a Class A chess player and an avid follower of sports, particularly boxing and baseball. In 1967, while living in San Miguel de Allende, Mexico, he organized a baseball team consisting of American expatriates like himself and Mexican locals.

With the advance he received from Grove Press for *Encyclopedia*, he traveled to India in 1968 and stayed for nearly five years. While there, he plunged into the study of Ayurveda, the traditional Hindu system of medicine based on diet, herbal treatment, and yogic breathing. During this period, while working on his second novel, he also wrote a number of travel essays which were published in *The East Village Other*, a popular New York City underground newspaper in the 1960s and early 1970s.

Horn returned to New York City in early 1973 and died in August of that year, a few months shy of his thirty-first birthday. The cause of death, reported by the city coroner, was "suffocation pending investigation." According to a couple of sources close to Horn, to the best of their knowledge, no investigation was ever conducted.

Acknowledgments

The publisher extends his profound thanks to the following for their generous financial support which helped to defray some of this edition's production costs:

Stephanie A., Kevin Adams, Riz Ahmad, R. E. Allen, Ben Anderson, John Alvey, Kate Alyssa, aurelius, j. t. baka, Diana Baldovino, Max Bang, Thomas Young Barmore Jr, Beans Marie, Melissa Beck, Joseph Benincase, Cameron Bennett, Jamie Benson-Zierfus, Kian S. Bergstrom, Sam Bertram, Carl W Bishop, Peter Blackett, Brian R. Boisvert, Bonriguez, Brian Booth, Ashley Bray, Lee Broadmore, David Brownless, Barry Buchanan, Josh Burrill, Chris Call, Gabriele Caredda, Morgan Carlson, Elaine M. Cassell, Scott Chiddister, Adam Cipriani, Chelsea Clifton, Greg Cobb, Joel Coblentz, C. Colla, Eric L. Collette, S COSTA, Parker & Malcolm Curtis, Robert Dallas, dcmalone, Edward De Vere, Joshua Doughty, Boaz David Dror, Mark A. Douglas, James Duncan, Andrew Eagle, Echo, Isaac Ehrlich, Myrhat Eliot, Evan M. Embrey, Pops Feibel, Steve Ferrezza, Mark Flemmich, Michael Flory, Tom Foster, old olaf fowles, Matt Frankie, Justin Gallant, Pierino Gattei, GMarkC, Jeff Goldsmith, B. F. Gordon Jr., Damian Gordon, The Grindilkin, Cassie LM-M and the Worry Clan, Gerald Groon, Everett Haagsma, Brian Hadley, Peter Halls, Alexann and Emory Hamlet, Sarah L. Hancock, Mahan Harirsaz, Erik Hemming, Ryan Ronald Hertel, isaac hoff, Yonina Hoffman, Dave Holets,

ACKNOWLEDGMENTS

Patrick Hollingsworth, J. Holmes, Todd Jailer, Peter J. Jansen,
Fred W Johnson, Kaitlyn A. Johnston, Arte Jones,
Jacob H Joseph, Kurt Johann Klemm, Jonathan Knell,
Tim Krcmarik, Stefan Kruger, Gen Kumana, Kyle, Mark Lamb,
Tim Latina, J. A. Lee, Leonore the Wanderer, Cari Liebenberg,
Gardner Linn, Nick Long, T Lowe, T. Lucas, Jim McElroy,
Fritz McFadden, Michelle Marie McKeehan,
Anneliese McKenna, Jack Mearns, William Messing,
Jason Miller, Jody L. Mock, Mohnach, Mark Molnar,
Spencer F Montgomery, Moog, Burke Morton, Gregory Moses,
Luke Mosher, Scott Murphy, NicholasHB, Heather O'Hearn,
Michael O'Shaughnessy, Joseph Ohlenbusch, Andrew Pearson,
Travis Pelkie, PhantomOfTheKnight, Michael Pfaff, Pedro Ponce,
PunkARTchick *Ruthenia*, Ned Raggett, Judith Redding,
Ryan C. Reeves, Evan Reznok, Robert Riley-Mercado,
Blair Roberts, Mike (DogFace) Robertson, Cassidy Rollins,
Andreas Rydin, Oliver S, Dave Samuelson, David W. Sanderson,
Ryan Scarcella, Florian Schiffmann, Norman Schlagenhauf,
James C Schoech, Connor Shirley, Brian K Skillin, Smell,
Ben Smith, Thadeus Hagan Smith, Kelly Snyder, Meera Sri,
Katina Stanley-Brown, Zane Nishimura Stillings, K. L. Stokes,
Lara Struttman, Felicia Sturdy, Keith Allen Tabb, Stephen Tabler,
Matt Tappert, S. Taushanoff, Tousedsa, Jennifer Trethewey,
trigonman3, Tim Tucker, Sydney Umaña, Nancy Usher,
Damon Van Demark, Yves Vandewoude, Dan Visel,
James R Walsh, R. A. Ward, Elizabeth Weitzman, Rachel Wells,
Christopher Wheeling, Isaiah Whisner, Bradley Wilken,
Charles Wilkins, Jeff Williams, Jeff Wilson, Marcel Wolf,
T.R. Wolfe, Casey Wright, Cyhiraeth "Rae" Ybarra,
Dylan and Wren Young, Yunus, BOBBY ZAMARRON,
The Zemenides Family, and Anonymous

Lightning Source UK Ltd.
Milton Keynes UK
UKHW041247070223
416605UK00001B/86